D0049471

PRISONER
B-3087

PRISONER B-3087

By
ALAN GRATZ

Based on the true story by RUTH and JACK GRUENER

SCHOLASTIC PRESS
NEW YORK

Copyright © 2013 by Alan Gratz, Ruth Gruener, and Jack Gruener

All rights reserved. Published by Scholastic Press, an imprint of Scholastic Inc., *Publishers since 1920.* SCHOLASTIC, SCHOLASTIC PRESS, and associated logos are trademarks and/or registered trademarks of Scholastic Inc.

No part of this publication may be reproduced, stored in a retrieval system, or transmitted in any form or by any means, electronic, mechanical, photocopying, recording, or otherwise, without written permission of the publisher. For information regarding permission, write to Scholastic Inc., Attention: Permissions Department, 557 Broadway, New York, NY 10012.

Library of Congress Cataloging-in-Publication Data

Gratz, Alan, 1972–
Prisoner B-3087 / by Alan Gratz. — 1st ed.
p. cm.
"Based on the true story by Ruth and Jack Gruener."
"While the story of Jack Gruener is true — and remarkable — this book is a work of fiction. As an author I've taken some liberties with time and events to paint a fuller and more representative picture of the Holocaust as a whole." — Afterword.
Includes a biographical afterword.
Summary: Based on the life of Jack Gruener, this book relates his story of survival from the Nazi occupation of Kraków, when he was eleven, through a succession of concentration camps, to the final liberation of Dachau.
ISBN 978-0-545-45901-3
1. Gruener, Jack — Juvenile fiction. 2. Jews — Poland — Kraków — Juvenile fiction.
3. Holocaust, Jewish (1939–1945) — Poland — Juvenile fiction. 4. Holocaust survivors — Poland — Juvenile fiction. 5. Kraków (Poland) — History — Juvenile fiction.
[1. Gruener, Jack — Fiction. 2. Jews — Poland — Kraków — Fiction. 3. Holocaust, Jewish (1939–1945) — Poland — Fiction. 4. Holocaust survivors — Fiction. 5. Kraków (Poland) — History — Fiction. 6. Poland — History — Fiction.] I. Title.
PZ7.G77224Pri 2013
813.6 — dc23
2012012460

ISBN 978-0-545-45901-3

12 11 10   15 16 17/0

Printed in the U.S.A.   23
First edition, March 2013
Book design by Natalie C. Sousa

For Jack,
who survived

PRISONER B-3087

KRAKÓW, POLAND

1939–1942

CHAPTER ONE

IF I HAD KNOWN WHAT THE NEXT SIX YEARS OF my life were going to be like, I would have eaten more.

I wouldn't have complained about brushing my teeth, or taking a bath, or going to bed at eight o'clock every night. I would have played more. Laughed more. I would have hugged my parents and told them I loved them.

But I was ten years old, and I had no idea of the nightmare that was to come. None of us did. It was the beginning of September, and we all sat around the big table in the dining room of my family's flat on Krakusa Street, eating and drinking and talking: my parents, my aunts and uncles, my cousins, and me, Jakob — although everybody called me by my Polish name, Yanek.

"'The Jews must disappear from Europe.' That's what Hitler said," Uncle Moshe said, reaching for another pastry. "I don't know how much more clear he could be."

I shivered. I'd heard Hitler, the German *fuehrer*, give speeches on the radio. *Fuehrer* meant "leader" in German. It was what the Germans called their president now. Hitler was always talking about the "Jewish menace" and how Germany and the rest of Europe should be "Jew free." I was a Jew, and I lived in Europe, and I didn't want to disappear. I loved my house and my city.

"The British and the French have already declared war on him," my father said. "Soon the Americans will join them. They won't let Germany roll over all of Europe."

"He's already annexed Austria and Czechoslovakia," said Uncle Abraham. "And now he invades Poland!"

My father sipped his coffee. "Mark my words: This war won't last more than six months."

My uncles argued with him, but he was my father, so I believed him.

"Enough politics," my mother said. She got up to clear the table, and my aunts helped her. "Yanek, why don't you put on a show for us? He built his own projector."

I ran to my room to get it. It wasn't a film projector like the one at the movie theater. It was a slide projector I'd made by mounting a lightbulb on a piece of wood and positioning wooden plates with lenses from magnifying glasses in front of it. I could show pictures on the wall, or do shadow-puppet shows. My cousins helped me hang a white sheet in the doorway of the sitting room, and when everyone was seated I plugged in the projector and clicked on the radio. I liked to have musical accompaniment, like a movie sound track. When the radio warmed up, I found a Count Basie song that was perfect and started my show.

Using cardboard cutouts of cowboys, Indians, stage-coaches, and horses I'd glued to sticks, I projected a shadow show about a sheriff in the American Wild West who had to protect his town from bandits. John Wayne Westerns were my favorite films, and I took all the best parts from his movies and made them one big story. My family laughed and cheered and called out to the characters like they were real. They loved my shows, and I loved putting them on for them. I was never prouder than when I got my father to laugh!

4

Maybe one day I would go to America and work in the movies. Aunt Gizela would often ruffle my wavy hair and say, "You look like a movie star, Yanek— with your dark-blond hair and big eyes."

I was just getting to the part where the bandit leader robbed the town bank and was squaring off for a shoot-out with the hero when the music on the radio stopped midsong. At first I thought the radio's vacuum tube had blown, but then a man's voice came on the radio.

"Ladies and gentlemen, we interrupt this broadcast with the news that the German army has reached Kraków."

"No!" my father said.

"So soon?" Uncle Moshe said. "It's been only six days! Where is the Polish army?"

I came out from behind the sheet in the doorway to listen. While the radio announcer talked about Polish forces withdrawing to Lodz and Warsaw, there was a big *BOOM*, and my mother's teacups rattled in their saucers. My cousins and I ran to the window to look outside. Dark smoke curled into the sky over the rooftops of Podgórze, our neighborhood. Someone cried out on the next street, and the church bells of Wawel Cathedral rang out in alarm.

It was too late. The Germans were here. If I had only known then what I know now, I would have run. I wouldn't have stopped to pack a bag, or say good-bye to my friends, or to even unplug my projector. None of us would have. We would have run for the woods outside of town and never looked back.

But we didn't. We just sat there in my family's flat, listening to the radio and watching the sky over Kraków turn black as the Germans came to kill us.

CHAPTER TWO

GERMAN SOLDIERS FILLED THE STREETS OF Kraków. They marched in their smart gray uniforms with their legs locked straight and thrown out in front of them the way ducks walk. It was silly, but eerie at the same time. There were so many of them, all marching in time together, their shiny green helmets and polished black jackboots glinting in the sun. Each of the soldiers wore a greatcoat and a pack on his back, and they carried rifles over their shoulders and bayonets at their sides.

I felt small in my little blue woolen jacket and pants and my simple brown cap. There were tanks too — panzers, they called them — great rumbling things with treads that clanked and cannons that swiveled on top.

We came out to watch. All of us: men, women, and children, Poles and Jews. We stood on the street corners and watched the Germans march through our city. Not all of Poland had fallen, the radio told us — Warsaw still held out, as did Brześć, Siedlce, and Lodz. But the Germans were our masters now, until our allies the British and the French arrived to drive them out.

"The Nazis won't be so bad," an old Polish woman on the sidewalk next to me said as I watched them. "I remember the Germans from the World War. They were very nice people."

But of course she could say that. She wasn't a Jew.

For weeks we tried to live our lives as though nothing had changed, as though an invading army hadn't conquered us. I went to school every day, my father and uncles and cousins still went to work, and my mother still went to the store. But things were changing. At school, the Polish boys wouldn't play soccer with me anymore, and no Poles or Germans bought shoes from my father's store. Food became scarce too, and more expensive.

Then one morning I walked to school and it was canceled. For good, I was told. No school for Jews.

The other children celebrated, but I was disappointed. I loved to read—any and all books. But especially books about America, and books about doctors and medicine.

I wandered the streets, watching the German soldiers and their tanks, the breadlines that stretched around the block. Winter was coming, and the men and women in line held their coats tight around them and stamped their feet to stay warm. When I went home at lunch-time, my father was there, which surprised me. He usually ate lunch at work. Uncle Moshe was with him at the table. My mother came out of the kitchen and worried over me.

"Are you sick, Yanek?" She put a hand to my fore-head. "Why are you home early from school?"

"It's closed," I told her, feeling depressed. "Closed for Jews."

"You see? You see?" Uncle Moshe said. He turned to my father, looking worked up. "First they close the schools. Next it will be your shoe store. My fur shop! And why not? No one will buy from us with Nazi soldiers telling people, 'Don't buy from Jews.'"

"But, if they close the shoe store, how will you make money?" I asked my father.

"Jews are not to make money!" Moshe said. "We have ration cards now for food. With *J*s all over them. *J* for Jew."

"This will pass," my father said. "They'll crack down for a time, and then things will get easier again. It's always the same. We just have to keep our heads down."

"Yes," Moshe said. He tapped the open newspaper between him and my father. "Jews must keep their heads down and not look Germans in the face. We can't speak unless spoken to. We can't walk on the main streets of our own city. We can't use the parks, the swimming pools, the libraries, the cinemas!"

Jews couldn't go to the movie theaters? No! I loved the movies! And the library too? Where would I get books to read if I wasn't allowed to go to school either? I hurried to Moshe's side to see what he was talking about. There, in the paper, were "New Rules for the Jews." My heart sank. It was true: no more parks, no more libraries, no more movie theaters. And there was to be a nightly curfew for all Jews, young and old. We were to be in our houses and off the streets by 9:00 P.M.

"And armbands. Armbands with the Star of David on them!" Uncle Moshe said. "They are marking us. Branding us like the cattle in those American pictures Yanek likes so much! Next they'll be taking all our money. Mina, tell your husband."

"What would you have us do, Moshe?" my mother said, putting her hands on my father's shoulders. "We haven't the money to leave. And even if we did, where would we go?"

My father reached up to hold my mother's hand. "We must not lose faith, Moshe."

"See how easy it is to keep your faith when the Nazis take it away along with everything else," Moshe told him.

My father smiled. "Let them take everything. They cannot take who we *are*."

I sat down at the table to eat, and my mother brought out a small tureen of tomato soup, a loaf of bread, and a wedge of cheese.

"So little?" I asked.

"It's the rationing. The groceries are all closed," Mother said.

"We'll make do," my father said. "We were spoiled before anyway."

I hadn't felt spoiled, but I didn't say anything. I just wished the Germans hadn't taken my lunch.

———◦———

Late that night, long after curfew, cries of "Fire!" woke us.

I ran from my bedroom, frightened. "What is it?" I cried when I saw my parents in the living room. "Is our building on fire? What do we do?"

"No," Father said. "It's the synagogue."

The synagogue was the place where we worshiped every Sabbath and where I was studying for my bar mitzvah. I leaned out the window and saw it down the street, engulfed in flames. My father hurried to put his coat on over his pajamas to go and help put out the fire, but a loud *crack!* from the street brought me and my parents to the window again. Another man wearing a coat and pajamas like my father lay dead in the middle of the street, a pool of darkness spreading beneath him, glinting in the streetlights. A German officer stood over him, his pistol still aimed at the dead man.

"Jews are reminded that under the new rules, anyone caught outside their homes after curfew will be shot on sight!" the officer yelled.

My father stood in the sitting room, his eyes on the door. My mother put a hand to his chest, then her head to his. Some unspoken communication passed between them, and in a few moments my father took his coat off again and sent me back to bed.

CHAPTER THREE

I WAS TWELVE YEARS OLD WHEN THE WALL began.

Podgórze, our neighborhood, was being walled up. From Zgody Square to the Podgórze market and down along Lasoty Place. The Nazis were walling us in.

I went out to see it. It was nearly three meters tall and made of brick. At the top it had rounded caps like the tops of tombstones. The wall stretched from one building corner to another, right across the street, cutting us off from the rest of Kraków. In the buildings that were part of the wall, they bricked up the windows and doors so no one could escape. There were only three ways in: a gate at Zgody Square, another at the market, and another on Lwowska Street.

I ran from gate to gate to gate, taking it all in. Podgórze was now the Jewish ghetto. All the Poles there who weren't Jews had to move out, and all the Jews who lived outside the ghetto in Kraków had to move *in*.

I watched them moving in. Wave after wave of them. Huge groups of Jews climbing out of trucks and going down Lwowska Street. There were men and women and children, families, teenagers, grandparents. They all wore Star of David armbands like us. Some of them wore the uniforms of the jobs they'd had too: policemen, postmen, nurses, trolley conductors. There were no jobs for Jews anymore. No jobs besides cleaning the toilets of German soldiers. My father and uncle had lost their shops, had their inventories seized by the Nazis, just as Uncle Moshe said they would.

The new Jews carried their luggage with them — everything they owned in the world — and they looked around with big, worried eyes at the buildings and streets of their new home. They were probably hoping that things would be better here than wherever it was they came from, but everything that had happened over the last year had taught us that things always got worse.

There were a few empty flats left by the departing Poles, but not nearly enough for all the new people. My parents came out onto the street and invited a family to come and live with us: the Laskis, a family of three with a seven-year-old boy named Aron. We gave them my bedroom, and I slept in the sitting room. Other families did the same.

Then, as the days went by and more and more Jews poured into the ghetto — not just from Kraków now, but from the villages and towns outside the city — we took in a second family, the Rosenblums, and a third, the Brotmans. The Germans even made it a rule: Every flat must hold at least four families. I no longer had my own bedroom, nor did my parents. The children had one room, and the adults were divided between my parents' bedroom and the sitting room. Only the kitchen was shared by all. There were fourteen of us in a flat that had been cozy for three.

All I ever wanted to do was get out of the house and go play with my friends. It was far too crowded at home. But my parents wouldn't let me go outside for fear I'd be taken up in a work gang. Any time the Germans had work to be done — like scrubbing toilets or helping build the wall — they grabbed Jews off the street to do it. Father was taken all the time. Sometimes Mother. The Nazis even took people out of the ghetto to work elsewhere in Kraków. Sometimes they never returned.

"This will all be over by summer," my father told us. "We'll just have to make do until then."

He was my father, and I wanted to believe him, but I wasn't so sure anymore. It was January 1941. The Germans ruled Kraków. I was twelve years old. And for the first time in my life, I had begun to doubt my father.

CHAPTER
FOUR

I HAD ALWAYS THOUGHT IT WOULD BE FUN TO have a brother or a sister. That is, until I spent a few months living in my little apartment with five other kids. The bickering, the fighting, the whining—you'd think that soldiers in the streets, and synagogues burning, and days with nothing more to eat than moldy potatoes would be more important than who got to play with the doll or who got to sleep by the window, but you'd be wrong.

The nights were the worst. I pulled my pillow and blanket out into the hall whenever the Rosenblum girls were arguing, which seemed like all the time now. I had to sleep on the floor, but I didn't mind so much. I would be sleeping on the floor here or there, and at least for now I had the whole hall to myself. If we had to take in another family, I thought bitterly, I'd probably have to share the hall too.

I was sound asleep one night when a creak in the hall woke me up. In the darkness, I saw the shape of a person.

"Who's there?" I asked, feeling my heart in my throat.

"Shhhh, Yanek. It's me," my father whispered. "I'm sorry I woke you. Go back to sleep."

Father had his coat on. He was going outside.

"Where are you going?" I asked him. "I want to go with you!"

"No. It's dangerous to be out after curfew."

"Then why are you going?" I was scared. I scrambled out from under my blanket. "Are you going to leave the ghetto?" Anyone caught trying to escape the ghetto was shot on sight.

"No, no. Go back to sleep, Yanek."

"No!" I wanted to help. My father had begun to look so tired lately. The work gangs and the lack of food made him look like he'd aged ten years in two. "I can help be your eyes. To look out for guards. I want to come with you!"

"Shhhh, Yanek. You'll wake everyone else." My father sighed. "All right. But not another word. We must be silent, you understand?"

I nodded and hurried to put on my coat. When I was ready, we slipped out the door and down the stairs. I had never been out this late before. The stairwell was dark and full of shadows. My heart still leaped at every little sound, even with my father there.

My father led me down the stairs like we were going to the building's furnace in the basement, but instead we went out through the back door, into the alley behind our building. Snow fell in big, thick flakes, muffling everything. It was so quiet you could hear the flakes hitting the snow that was already on the ground. *Tick. Tick. Tick tick.*

I followed my father through the silent alley. Our footprints left tracks in untrodden snow. I looked behind me, suddenly worried that we were leaving a trail that would be easy to follow. But the falling snow was already covering our tracks. I prayed for more of it, even though more would mean new work details — for my father and other Jewish men — to clear it in the morning.

We had to cross at Jozefinska Street, which meant we would be out in the open. Down the block, a German soldier in a greatcoat, scarf, and hat cupped his hands to his face to light a cigarette. My father put a hand to my chest, and we flattened ourselves against the wall in the shadow of an apartment building. I watched the German soldier breathe out a long cloud of smoke. The red ember of his cigarette glowed in the darkness. Where was he from? What was his name? Did he have a family? Children, like me? Did he hate Jews the way Hitler did? Had he ever killed a man?

The Nazi rubbed his hands together, stomped his feet to clear the snow and cold from them, and walked around the corner, out of sight.

"Now," my father whispered, and we hurried across the street, our feet crunching so loudly in the quiet night air I thought everyone on the block must hear us. I'd crossed that street a hundred times—a thousand times—but it had never felt so wide, the other side so far away. When we reached the alley across the street we stopped, leaning against a wall again while we caught our breaths and listened to see if anyone had heard us. The only sound was the falling of the snow. *Tick. Tick. Tick tick.*

My father led me a short way on, and I began to realize where we were going: Uncle Abraham's bakery! The Nazis had let him keep it to bake bread for the soldiers. As we pushed on the door to go inside, something caught: A towel was stuffed into the crack along the floor. As soon as we were inside, I understood why.

Bread. The wonderful, beautiful smell of bread! The aroma alone made my stomach growl. I had learned to live with hunger, but now that my body knew there was fresh baked bread to be had, it could barely contain itself. I shook with anticipation. My father replaced the towel under the door, and we made our way down the dark corridor to the ovens. Uncle Abraham and Aunt Fela had covered every window and door with towels, sheets, blankets, anything that would block out the light—and the smell.

"Oskar!" Uncle Abraham said to my dad when we found them. He hugged my father, and I ran to where Aunt Fela was pulling racks of bread from the oven.

"And I see you brought a helper," Aunt Fela said. "Hello, Yanek." She smiled at me, but I only had eyes for the bread. Golden brown loaves that glistened and steamed in the cool air. I felt my mouth water.

Fela laughed. "Take one."

"*After* we work," my father said, and my heart burst. How could I possibly wait? He turned to my uncle.

"What can we do? Are you firing both ovens?" my father asked.

"Only one for bread," Uncle Abraham said. He opened the second oven to show it was empty. "In this one, we're burning wet wood, to help cover the smell of the bread with the smoke. We weren't able to save enough flour to bake in both ovens all the time anyway. We must make it last. Another month? Another two? Another year?"

"Spring," my father said. "The British and the French will be here by then."

Uncle Abraham shrugged. "It may be the Russians get here first. The peace can't last." Seventeen days after Germany had invaded Poland from the west, the Soviet Union had invaded from the east. Poland was split right down the middle, and the Germans and Russians had promised not to fight each other. For now. "In the meantime, we'll bake when we can. But if the Nazis find out . . ."

"Come, let's get to it," my father said. "Yanek and I will feed the fires."

We worked into the wee hours of the morning—Father and I feeding wood and coal into the ovens, Uncle Abraham making dough, Aunt Fela pulling those delectable loaves from the racks and putting them in sacks.

"We must get you back before light," Uncle Abraham said at last. "Here. Take three sacks apiece. That should be enough to sell on Krakusa Street, plus one sack for yourself."

A whole sack of bread, just for us! I almost moaned at the thought of such a feast.

"Moshe is coming by tomorrow to pick up sacks to sell to the families on Wegierska Street," Abraham said. "And Dawid and Sala tomorrow night, to sell to Rekawka Street."

"How much per loaf?" Father asked.

Abraham shrugged. "Five zloty, perhaps."

Five zloty! A loaf of bread usually cost no more than half a zloty!

"I hate to be so mercenary, but the price of flour has gone up too."

"You can still buy flour?" Father asked.

"There are boys who have already found holes in the wall, ways to get out. They can buy things on the other side. For a price," Aunt Fela said.

"These new Jews, they have more money too. They can afford it," Abraham said. "Now go, before it's light."

"Enjoy your bread, Yanek," Aunt Fela said. She kissed my forehead, and Abraham and my father hugged each other good-bye.

When we left, it was still dark outside, and still snowing. There would be more patrols, and the ghetto would soon be waking. There was no time to waste.

"Once more then, Yanek, to home. And then we shall have fresh bread for breakfast. How does that sound?"

"Delicious," I said.

Father put a hand on my shoulder and squeezed it. "We just have to survive the winter, Yanek, and then everything will be better. You'll see."

I still worried he was wrong, but fresh bread made me forget all my troubles. For a little while, at least.

CHAPTER FIVE

1942 CAME, BUT THE BRITISH DIDN'T. NOR DID the French. They were too busy fighting the Germans in the west. The radio talked about the fighting in Denmark and Norway and Belgium and the Netherlands, but since it was a German station, they always said they were winning. Uncle Moshe said we couldn't trust anything we heard, but he listened to every word anyway, just like the rest of us.

All I cared about was getting out of our crowded house for some freedom and fresh air, but my parents were still worried I'd be snatched up by the Nazis. The snow was still thick on the ground, with more falling every day, and Jews were put to work shoveling it off the streets. The Nazis also took Jews away to work in Kraków's factories. Some of the truckloads of Jews never came back, but nobody knew what happened to them. My parents didn't want to take any chances one way or another, so I had to stay in our building at all times.

I took my ball into the hallway outside our apartment and practiced kicking it against the wall until mean old Mrs. Immerglick across the hall came out and yelled at me to stop. I was just about to go downstairs to the basement to play when I heard a scream from one of the lower floors. Then footsteps. Lots of footsteps. A door smashing. More screams.

I ran back inside our flat. "Mama! Mama!" I called to my mother. "Something is happening in the building!"

Everyone staying in our apartment came together in the sitting room. We listened as the screams and crashes grew closer. I felt sick. I wished my father were there with us, but he had gone out to stand in line for our vegetable rations.

THUMP THUMP THUMP. Someone pounded on our door, and we all jumped.

"Open up, on authority of the Judenrat!"

Everyone looked to my mother. It was our flat, after all. But she just watched the door with big, round eyes.

My heart was racing. What should we do? What *could* we do?

"Mama?" I said.

THUMP THUMP THUMP.

"Open the door or we'll break it down!" said another voice, this time in German. A Nazi.

"Mama," I said, "if we don't open up, they'll shoot us!"

My mother stared at the door. None of the other parents made a move.

I had to do something. I hurried to the door and unlocked it, and a German officer and a Judenrat police officer pushed past me down the hall. The Judenrat were the Jews the Nazis put in charge of the ghetto, and they had special police officers who had to take orders from the Nazis.

"When we tell you to open the door, open the door!" the German officer told the adults. The families huddled together, hugging one another tight. "Do you have jewels? Gold? A radio?" he demanded.

My mother didn't answer. She just stared at the Nazi and trembled. He was getting madder, I could tell. The officer took a step toward my mother, and I spoke up.

"In the kitchen!" I said.

The German turned to look at me with his cold blue eyes, then nodded to the Jewish policeman, who carried a sack.

"Your valuables," the officer said. "Now. Or you will all be taken away."

Someone screamed across the hall. Old Mrs. Immerglick and her family were being dragged away by German soldiers. Her son, a man my father's age, had blood running down his forehead.

"Give it to them!" I yelled. "Give them anything they want!"

The other families in our flat scrambled to give the Nazi officer everything they had squirreled away: little bits of jewelry, a pocket watch, a handful of zloty. The member of the Judenrat came out of our kitchen with his sack stuffed with more than just our radio and went into the bedrooms, looking for anything more of value.

The German officer pulled the necklace from my mother's neck, and twisted her wedding ring from her finger. She flinched when he did it, but she didn't say a word.

"This flat can stay," the German officer said, pocketing my mother's jewelry. "But next time, open the door more quickly, or we will send you to the east with the rest."

"Yes, sir. We will, sir!" I said.

The two men left, and we all stood frozen, listening to the shouts and sobs above us and below us. Out on the streets, two big gray military trucks pulled up, and Jews from our apartment building and all the buildings around us were herded into them by German soldiers. They carried nothing with them. No suitcases, no extra clothes, no food, no personal belongings. Wherever they were going, they would have to do without.

Something clattered in the hall outside. The doors to our flat and the Immerglicks' apartment were still open. I could see an overturned table and lamp in their flat, but nothing more. Why had the Immerglicks and the families living with them been taken, and we hadn't? The officer said it was because we gave them our valuables, but the Immerglicks had a radio and jewelry and zloty, just like us. The Germans had taken the Immerglicks for no more reason than that they felt like it.

A shot rang out in the street, and we all jumped again.

"Yanek," Mr. Rosenblum whispered. "The door."

I glanced at my mother, but she was a million miles away. Her eyes were focused on the rug at our feet, her face empty of emotion. I don't know if she had even heard the shot. I tiptoed down the entrance hall and closed the door, flipping the lock with a *click*. It didn't make me feel any safer.

—⬩—

When the trucks in the street were full, they pulled away. We never heard where they went. My father could have been on one of them, for all I knew.

My mother sat at the table, her mind still elsewhere. At this time of day, she would usually be in the kitchen, preparing whatever rations we had for lunch, but that was no use now. Our cupboards had been cleared out in the raid. We had nothing to eat.

The other families retreated to their rooms to see what had been taken and what was left. The Rosenblum girls wailed like they were trying to outdo each other in volume, so I slipped out into the hall. The door to the Immerglicks' flat was still open, and someone was inside. It was Mr. Tatarka, from down the hall. When he heard the *click* of the door behind me he whirled. One of the Immerglicks' nice cushioned sitting-room chairs was in his hands. He opened his mouth to say something, got flustered, then hurried out past me. He took the chair with him.

I walked the hallway on my floor, looking in at the empty rooms. Four flats, sixteen families, all gone. Only two had their doors shut — us and the Tatarkas. Five flats were empty on the floor above us, but only three on the top floor. Maybe the Germans got tired of walking up all those steps.

I went back to the stairs and realized for the first time that there was another set of stairs going up, even though this was the top floor. I'd never had any friends on the top floor, so I had gone up only once or twice in the past to run an errand. I stared down the stairwell, listening for a new invasion of Germans, but everything was quiet and still. I climbed the extra flight of stairs.

There was a big steel door at the top. I opened it a crack and looked outside. The roof! This door led out onto the roof! How had I not known this was here? But then, even if I had known, my parents would never have let me come up here. Not in the past, when things like bedtimes and homework and safe places to play had been important. None of that mattered now, and I pushed my way outside and stood on the roof of our building.

It was flat and covered with gravel. Pipes and conduits stuck up out of the roof here and there. The roof's edges, a little more than half a meter all the way around, were plastered with black tar. Strangest of all was a small wooden shack built up against the big brick chimney. It had a thin wooden door, and when I went inside, I found heaps of garbage and feathers and bird droppings. A pigeon coop! Mr. Immerglick's pigeon coop, probably. When I was a little boy, all I knew about the old man who lived across the hall was that he loved pigeons, but I had never imagined he kept a coop on the roof. The pigeons were all gone now, just like Mr. Immerglick; he died a year before the Nazis came. But this shack on the roof . . . if it was repaired a little, cleaned up, maybe had some electricity running to it from the power lines that came into the building from the roof . . . My mind was racing.

I ran back downstairs as fast as I could and burst into my flat.

"Mama!" I cried.

I found my mother in the kitchen, hugging my father. He was alive!

He broke away from her when I came running in, worried.

"What is it, Yanek?" he asked. "Are they coming back?"

"No! No. I want to show you something I found. Come quick!"

My parents followed me up the stairs, walking when I wanted them to run. Finally I pulled them out onto the roof and showed them the pigeon coop.

"Don't you see? With a little work, we could live here!"

"Leave our flat?" Father asked.

"Just the three of us," I told them. "It's so crowded downstairs. Here we can have a space all to ourselves. We can scrub the floor and the walls, clean it up. And I can wire up a light—the light from my projector! And a hot plate, for cooking on. There's no bathroom, but we could always go back downstairs for that. And in the winter, we'll have the chimney to keep us warm."

"I don't know, Yanek," my father said.

My mother hadn't come inside the coop. Instead she stood just outside, staring back at the big steel door that opened onto the roof.

"We can bring up chairs," I told my father. "And a mattress, and —"

"Bars," my mother said. It was the first thing I'd heard her say since the Nazis burst into our flat. "Can you put bars . . . on the door?" She stared at it, but I could tell her thoughts were still downstairs, reliving the invasion of our home.

My father came out of the coop and put his arm around my mother's shoulders.

"Yes, Mina. We will fix up the coop and live here, and we will put bars on the door. Yanek and I will see to it."

We gave our flat to the Rosenblums. The Brotmans were already moving into the Immerglicks' apartment across the hall. All the empty flats in our building would soon be overflowing with families as more Jews were marched in through the gates. But for a short time at least, we would all live like normal people again.

While my father and I worked to clean the coop, my mother sat on the roof and sewed hidden pockets into the linings of our coats. Inside them, she hid all the money and valuables we had left. She never said another word though, all that day.

Father and I found four heavy steel bars in the basement. By sundown, we lifted the last of them onto the door to the roof. They slid into place so we could take them off to go out, but so that no one from inside the stairs could push through.

"There," I told my mother. "No one will be able to break in ever again."

CHAPTER SIX

THE PIGEON COOP BECAME OUR HOME, AND NO Nazi was the wiser.

I was old enough that my parents couldn't keep me inside all the time now. I took my mother's place in line for our rations, and sometimes my father and I were pulled off the street to work outside the ghetto. But each day we returned to our little sanctuary on the roof and slid the steel bars down tight to protect us. Mother began to talk again, and to smile, but every now and then I would catch her staring at the door to the roof, and I knew what she was thinking.

The home invasions continued without warning, slowly bleeding everything of value the ghetto still hoarded. And once a week — on the Sabbath — the Nazis would conduct "Resettlements," when they came and took more people away. Thousands at a time, pushed into trucks and taken to villages "in the east." Some who were taken escaped and sneaked back to the ghetto, and they told stories of camps where Jews were worked to death. My father told me not to listen to the rumors, but we were still careful to bar the big steel door at the top of the stairs every night, and every time we heard the cries and screams of a new Resettlement we huddled in fear.

I was almost thirteen years old now, and it was hard to remember any other life—except for my daydreams of food. *Bigos* stew, with meat and mushrooms and cabbage. Roast chicken. Cucumber salad. Pierogi filled with potatoes, cheese, and onions, fried in butter. Cheesecake, apple tarts. I would have traded a week's worth of rations just to have another pot of my mother's delicious tomato soup. With each passing day I grew thinner and thinner, until hunger was my constant companion. I longed for nighttime, and the blessed relief sleep brought. The only time I didn't think about eating was when I was asleep.

One cold February day, the director of the Judenrat called for a ghetto-wide meeting in Zgody Square, and my father and I went to hear what he had to say. The director was not a popular man. The members of the Judenrat were hated throughout the ghetto for working with the Nazis. But any man the Nazis assigned to the Judenrat who refused was shot or hanged, so I didn't see what choice they had. Some of the Judenrat police enjoyed their new jobs too much, it was true, but there were others who tried to do what the Germans told them without making things worse for their fellow Jews.

The square was crowded, but not everyone in the ghetto was there. Not nearly. The director could tell this too. He checked his watch one last time and bent forward to speak into the microphone. "When I call for a meeting, all of you must come!" he told us. "Tell your neighbors. Hiding away will not help!"

I glanced nervously at my father.

"We're afraid we'll be taken away!" someone yelled.

"Or shot and killed in the street!" someone else said.

The director signaled for everyone to settle down. "My friends, I come to you with a terrible request, but one which I have no choice but to accede to. The Nazis have ordered me to give them seven thousand Jews, to be deported from the Kraków ghetto tomorrow morning."

The crowd came alive with murmurs and sobs and shouts. *Seven thousand Jews!* I thought, trying to comprehend a number so big. There had been Resettlements going on all the while, but nothing on this scale. Never so many people.

"We can do nothing about this! Seven thousand people *will* be deported! But we can choose who will go and who will remain."

"*You* can choose, you mean!" someone yelled.

"The Germans need good, healthy workers here in the ghetto," the director said.

"You call this healthy?" a man cried. "I haven't eaten meat in a year!"

Others in the crowd shouted angrily that they were starving. I nodded, feeling my own hunger pangs.

"If we prove ourselves useful to the German war effort, they will take fewer of us away. They will keep us here, and keep us alive!" the director said. "We must therefore think carefully about who we send away, and who remains. We must give them those who cannot work."

More murmuring among the crowd. "Who can he mean?" I asked my father. Everyone in the ghetto worked. Even my mother had been taken to the factories when she was caught out on the streets.

"My friends," the director said, "I must reach out my arms and beg: Mothers and fathers, give me your children!"

The crowd in the square erupted with rage. Angry shouts were raised from every mouth. Fists shook in the air. An empty green bottle flew through the air and shattered at the base of the stage where the director stood. I was scared but I felt angry too. I held on to my father's arm.

"They go to a better place!" the director said, ducking a rock. "The children will be sent to resettlement camps!"

"Work camps!" someone near me yelled.

"*Death camps!*" another person cried.

"*I am trying to save lives!*" the director roared. "Do you understand? Which is better, that forty thousand of us remain, or that the whole population perish? We must choose!"

"They can't do this," I told my father. "Why does he get to choose who goes and who stays?"

The reality was starting to hit me: I was going to be sent to a camp. I was going to be sent away from my mother and father. Away from my home!

The crowd yelled and argued with the director, surging toward the stage. My father put his hands on my shoulders and steered me away. "Come, Yanek. Let's go."

I couldn't believe what I'd heard. "Papa, how can he ask such a thing?"

"Because the Nazis have promised not to take him and his family, and people will do anything to protect their families. He should know that better than anyone."

"I don't want to go! Don't let them take me," I said. I could feel myself trembling, but I didn't want to let on just how deeply terrified I was.

"They won't," my father told me. "I'll protect you." He smiled. "Besides, tomorrow you will no longer be a child, will you, Yanek? Do you think I've forgotten it's your birthday?"

To be honest, I had thought he would forget. Mother too. There was nothing to mark the days now except the Sabbath, and we had to observe it in secret, anyway. But I knew. Tomorrow was my thirteenth birthday — the day I would officially become a man.

"Your mother and I have said nothing because how can we possibly hold a bar mitzvah for you? If we're caught celebrating it, we'll be killed."

I nodded. I'd been looking forward to my bar

mitzvah for as long as I could remember, but now it wasn't going to happen. It couldn't.

"Still," my father said like he could read my mind, "we will celebrate it."

"But how?"

"Tonight," Father told me, "go to sleep in your clothes."

That night, I lay awake in my clothes, tossing and turning. *My bar mitzvah*, I thought.

A bar mitzvah is the ceremony in which a Jewish boy becomes a man—the first time he reads aloud from the Torah. Usually all of my school friends and aunts and uncles and cousins would have come to see me read in the synagogue. There would have been a kiddush after the service, with challah rolls, potatoes, chicken—my stomach growled just thinking about it. But of course there was no synagogue anymore, and no challah rolls or potatoes or chicken.

A few hours must have passed before I heard my father stir. My mother too. I sat up on my mattress and waited while my father pulled on his overcoat.

"We must be quiet," Father whispered. "Like the night we went to Abraham's bakery."

I nodded and stood. My mother came to me and hugged me tight. "Come back to me a man, my Yanek. Only come back."

"I will," I promised her.

Mother kissed me on the cheek and walked us to the steel door that protected our rooftop home. She slid the metal bars back in place when we were through, and we made our way quietly down the dark stairs of our apartment building. Tonight there was no snow, but it was cold. We could see the breath from our noses. I pushed my hands down into my pockets as far as they would go and wished I hadn't outgrown my gloves.

Father led me through the back alleys again. Once, we turned a corner to find another night stalker. It was a Jewish boy carrying a bag of something over his shoulder — food, I guessed, smuggled through some hole in the wall — and all three of us gasped. When it was clear none of us was a Nazi we all hurried on our way without a word, but we were even more cautious than before. Our path took us toward the wall, and at first I wondered if Father meant to take us out. We climbed into an old abandoned warehouse building that stood along the wall at Dabrowki Street. Almost every window was broken and open to the sighing wind, and the rotted wooden floor had holes in it. There were stairs at the back, narrow and rickety, and occasionally missing a tread, and down we went into the basement. It wasn't exactly where I had imagined celebrating one of the biggest milestones of my life, but I followed along without a word.

There were men in the basement waiting for us. My uncles Abraham and Moshe, my cousin Dawid, two more men I recognized as friends of my father, and three more I didn't know. One of them held a set of Torah scrolls in a burlap sack, saved, perhaps, from one of the ghetto's synagogues before it burned to the ground.

The men whispered hello. Ordinarily my uncles and cousins would have embraced us and talked, but everyone was too scared of being out after curfew to say anything more. My stomach grumbled, loud in the silent basement, reminding me that now that I was awake I should be finding it some food.

The stairs creaked behind us, and we all turned. My heart was in my throat. If we were caught down here, together, with the Torah in hand, I would never become a man. I would be shot dead on sight. But the shoes we saw coming down were not the glistening boots of an SS officer. They were the brown leather soles of Mr. Tatarka from down the hall.

"Now we are ten men," my father whispered. He smiled at me. "And soon we shall be eleven. I'm sorry we did not have more time for your studies, Yanek. Just do your best."

The Torah scrolls were taken out and unrolled so I could read from them. My Hebrew was rough. Before the Nazis, I would have been at the synagogue once or twice a week ahead of time, practicing for this. But of course that was impossible now. I muddled through, and if God or man heard anything amiss, neither of them called me on it.

When I was finished, my father chanted a blessing over me in the place of our rabbi, who had been killed by the Germans. He prayed in Hebrew, then spoke in Polish.

"Yanek, my son," he said, looking at me solemnly, "you are a man now, with all the duties of an adult under Jewish law. You are now responsible for your own sins, but also for your own goodness. Remember what the Talmud teaches: Life is but a river. It has no beginning, no middle, no end. All we are, all we are worth, is what we do while we float upon it — how we treat our fellow man. Remember this, and a good man you will be."

"I will, Father," I said. I had waited for this day, looked forward to it for years. Suddenly it didn't matter that we weren't in a synagogue, that we didn't have a feast waiting for us afterward. The smile on my father's face filled me with pride.

The men all shook my hand and wished me *mazel tov* before hurrying off.

"They're leaving tonight, most of them," Moshe told us. "Trying to escape before tomorrow's Deportation. Seven thousand! Never so many."

"We'll survive," my father told him. "Come to our pigeon coop and hide with us."

"Oskar and his river," Uncle Moshe said. "You should talk some sense into him now that you're a man, Yanek. The man who falls asleep on the river drowns."

CHAPTER SEVEN

"JEWS OF KRAKÓW!" THE ANNOUNCEMENT blared from speakers. "Get up! Get out! Get moving! Seven thousand volunteers are needed for the resettlement camps!"

The asked-for volunteers had not appeared in Zgody Square the next morning, and the Germans were not happy. Just after dawn they drove through the streets of the ghetto in trucks with big speakers on them, yelling at us to come out.

"It will be worse for you if you hide!" they called. "Come out now, and all will be forgiven."

I didn't believe them. None of us did. Uncle Moshe, Aunt Gizela, and my cousin Zytka were all there with us. They had decided to come hide in our pigeon coop.

So had the rest of my aunts and uncles and cousins. There were twelve of us, all crammed inside the little shack on the roof. It was too crowded, but there was no way we would turn them away. Everyone was afraid of this new announcement, and we had seen too many smaller Resettlements to take it lightly. At least all of us pressed together in the coop helped keep us warm — we couldn't start a fire, or the smoke would give us away.

A gunshot rang out. *Crack!* A woman screamed. *Pop-pop-pop-pop-pop-pop* went a machine gun. I scrambled to the little window in our coop, where we'd hung a blanket to hide us.

"*Yanek, no,*" my mother whispered, but I had to see. Across the street was a building that had been turned into a hospital, and I watched through a hole in the blanket as the Nazis pushed sick people out the door and down the steps. Some of them were too weak to walk and collapsed on the pavement. They cried out piteously.

"What's happening?" Moshe asked.

My heart was in my throat, but I managed to answer. "Sick people, old people — they're taking them out of the hospital."

"They can't be taking them to the work camps or for resettlement," Moshe said. His voice was quiet, but urgent. "They would never take the sick and the old away to work. They're taking them to die — and anyone else with them!"

As I watched, the Nazis walked up behind the sick people from the hospital and started to shoot. Bodies fell on bodies, a great pile of them in the street. They fell with terrible screams.

I pulled away from the window, unable to watch anymore.

"No," I said. "They're not taking them away. They're shooting them right here."

Not even Uncle Moshe had anything to say to that. My mother reached for my hand and pulled me back to her. We sat like that for hours, listening to the gunshots and the screams in the street, my younger cousins huddled next to their mothers, weeping on and off quietly.

I was terrified just like they were, but I wasn't going to cry. I was a man now, I reminded myself. I was a man, and I wanted to *do* something. Something to stop the Nazis. To save my family. I asked myself over and over again what I could do to help, but I had no answer.

Shunk-shunk. The big metal door to the roof rattled — someone was trying to come through! I held my breath, listening. *Shunk-shunk. Shunk-shunk.* Would the steel bars hold? Would whoever was on the other side start shooting? I watched my mother's eyes grow wide again, watched her chest heave as she breathed faster and faster. She looked like she might scream, which would give us away for sure. My father hugged her close, holding her face to his shoulder. *Shunk-shunk. Shunk-shunk.* I waited for a gunshot, waited, waited — but then, for whatever reason, the rattling stopped, and whoever it was went away. We held still, none of us daring to breathe, waiting for someone to try to come through again, but an hour passed, and then another, and another, and no one came back.

That evening, the trucks drove through the streets again with a new message for us.

"Jews of Kraków! Unless everyone comes to Zgody Square for selection, this ghetto will be liquidated! If you do not come out of your houses by six P.M., every one of you will be shot on sight when we find you!"

"'*Liquidated,*' do you hear that?" Uncle Abraham said. "Liquidated, like it's a business decision. They would get rid of us like so many old pairs of shoes."

"We should go," Moshe said. He stood. "You heard them. They will kill us if we don't."

"They will kill us if we do!" I said.

"They said they will liquidate the ghetto only if we do not come out. By hiding, we seal our death warrant," Moshe said.

"No!" I said. I could feel my pulse racing. "We can't trust them! It's a trick. I know it is. It's a trick to get us to come out of our hiding place!"

"You're still a boy, Yanek, even if you've had your bar mitzvah. Listen to me, all of you. If we stay here and are found, we'll be shot," Moshe argued. He opened the door to the coop. "We have to go now. If we do what they say, they may let us live."

My uncles and cousins started arguing about it. Dawid agreed with Moshe. Abraham wanted to stay. My aunts argued too, and the younger children started to cry. I looked to my parents to see what they wanted, but my mother's face was still buried in my father's shoulder, and he was comforting her. Tears welled up in my eyes. I wasn't a boy. Not anymore. Not after my bar mitzvah. Not after a year in the Kraków ghetto. I knew I had to be a grown-up now, for my parents. For everyone.

I pushed past Uncle Moshe and marched to the big metal door. I yanked off the steel bars and flung the door open with a *clang*.

"There!" I said. "Go! If you want to leave so badly, if you want to hand yourselves over to those killers, then do it right now! But I'm not. I've seen what the Nazis think of us. How they treat us. We all have. So they kill us if they find us here. If we go down there on our own they will most certainly kill us! At least if we hide out here there is a *chance* they won't find us. That's a chance I'm willing to take."

My outburst shut everyone else up. They all stared at one another without speaking until my father rose.

"Yanek speaks with the wisdom of the prophet Isaiah," he said softly, then quoted, "'Come, my people . . . and shut your doors behind you; hide your-selves for a little while until the wrath is past.'" He cleared his throat and looked around. "Mina and I are staying too."

One by one, the others agreed, until even Uncle Moshe sat down and was quiet. I closed the door and slid the steel bars back in place, making sure they were tight. Night fell, and with it came more gunshots, more screams from the streets below. The Deportation lasted for two days. But on the third day, when the sun rose, there were no more trucks in the streets, no more gunshots, no more Nazis. They did not liquidate the entire ghetto, as they had promised. Once their quota was filled, they went away again.

Seven thousand Jews had been collected and taken away to die, but we were not among them.

CHAPTER EIGHT

AFTER THE DEPORTATION, THE WAILING OF OLD women could be heard from nearly every window and door in the ghetto. Seven thousand husbands and fathers, wives and mothers, brothers and sisters, and children had been taken to their deaths — or so we heard from survivors.

Rumors were whispered in the streets: that shootings in the woods were too much trouble for the Nazis. Now they were gassing Jews to death in trucks and boiling their bodies to make soap, or so it was said. The thought of that made my stomach turn. There were more Deportations, but for a time they were smaller selections, like those that had come before, and my existence in the ghetto — it wasn't a life, just an existence—went back to what it was. Those who could work were not taken away, and so, reluctantly, my father and I showed up for work details every morning. I was assigned to a tailor shop, and the work was manageable, but it seemed as if my former life—school, friends, time to play and read—belonged to another world entirely.

One afternoon after work, I made a fateful decision. I went by a friend's house instead of going directly back to my family's rooftop hideaway. If I had gone straight home, if I had gone out to get our rations with my mother and father, things might have turned out very differently than they did.

The streets of the ghetto were empty when I finally headed home that day. The emptiness could only mean one thing—another Deportation. When the Nazis came looking for Jews to deport, all the people who lived on the streets found places to hide. They had to, or they'd be taken. Men and women with homes to go to put their heads down and hurried there by whatever back alleys and side streets they could. I skirted down Limanowskiego Street, ready to duck behind a busted-up piece of furniture or hide in a pile of old rags if I heard the Nazis coming.

I was almost home when I heard the bark of German officers around the corner and the shuffling of shoes on pavement. I scanned the area for any place I could hide, but there wasn't one. I squeezed myself into a corner on the other side of a short set of stairs to an apartment building and tried to disappear into the shadows.

The Nazi officers marched by in the street in front of me. All they had to do was turn their heads to see me, but they kept their eyes forward, followed by a ragtag group of Jews who were being deported. I watched them go by, a few hundred or so, their heads bent low and every one of them silent as the grave.

Wait—there. In the middle of the crowd. I froze.

Was that my mother and father?

I stood on my toes, trying to see into the mass of people, but the angle had changed. I was standing in plain sight now, my head and shoulders well over the top of the short flight of stairs, but I didn't care. Were my parents in that Deportation? Maybe I'd just seen a couple who resembled them.

I wanted to scream. I almost ran to the column of marching Jews to call my parents' names, to find out if that was really them. But the sight of the German SS officers bringing up the rear stopped me. If my parents weren't being marched right now, I'd be caught and never see them again. But if it *was* them —

As soon as the prisoners and their guards were past, I dashed out from behind the stairs and ran all the way home. I burst through the door to our apartment building and raced up the stairs and pounded on the big metal door to our rooftop hideaway. The bars were still over the door, which was good news. That meant someone was still up there. I prayed it was my mother and called through the door to her as I pounded away. Behind the door I heard the steel bars being lifted and I stopped knocking, my heart racing. The door opened, and my cousin Sala stood behind it, tears running down her face.

"No," I said. *"No."*

My knees went weak, and I closed my eyes against the truth that was coming.

"Yanek," Sala said. "Yanek, thank God you're all right."

"Where are they?" I demanded, even though I already knew. "Sala, where are my parents?"

"I'm so sorry, Yanek. The Nazis grabbed them as they were coming back from buying bread. I saw them taken, right there in the street in front of the building."

I staggered through the door and into the pigeon coop that had been our home, our sanctuary, for more than a year. It was totally empty.

I fell to my knees and sobbed. Sala put her hand on my shoulder, but I could barely feel it. Mama. Papa. They were gone. My family was gone. I felt like my heart was being wrenched out of my chest.

The emptiness of the pigeon coop weighed heavy on me. I was the only one left. How would I survive? *Why* should I survive? *Maybe I should just go and give myself to the Nazis*, I thought with bitterness, with defeat.

No, I thought.

I wiped the tears from my eyes with the back of my sleeve. My parents would not want that for me. In the place of my pain, I felt the stirring of determination.

I would not give up. I would not turn myself in. No matter what the Nazis did to me, no matter what they took from me, I would survive.

I was thirteen years old, and my parents were gone.

I was all alone in the world, but I would survive on my own.

PLASZÓW
CONCENTRATION CAMP

1942–1943

CHAPTER NINE

THE NAZIS SNATCHED ME UP ONE DAY WHEN I was at work.

I was still working at the tailor shop in Kraków, hoping that would save me from the Deportations. But my work there ended up being the reason I was taken. The tailor shop at Plaszów, a nearby labor camp, needed more workers, we were told. So we were taken.

I had known this day would come. In the days and weeks after my parents were deported, the rest of my family had gone too. Uncle Moshe had disappeared while on a work detail. Uncle Abraham and Aunt Fela were pulled from their home in a Deportation. Cousins Sala, Dawid, and their two boys while in line for bread. Aunt Gizela and little Zytka went for a voluntary selection in Zgody Square, in hopes that the Nazis meant what they said about resettlement. By the summer of 1942, only I remained — the sole member of my family left in the Kraków ghetto. I thought I'd be ready for it when they took me away, but I wasn't.

They loaded us into a truck, and all the horror stories I'd heard suddenly became real to me. Were the Nazis lying to us? Were we going to die? Were we really being taken to the woods to be shot? I panicked, looking for a way out — out of the truck, out of Plaszów, out of this nightmare that had already swallowed my parents and everyone I loved. But just outside the truck were Nazis with machine guns. They didn't even have to point them at me for the message to be clear: It was either go where this truck was taking me or die here on the streets of Kraków. I had sworn to myself I would survive, so I made the choice that kept me alive, if only for the moment, and took a seat on the truck.

The women I worked with begged to be able to tell their families back in the ghetto good-bye, to tell them where they were being taken, but the Nazis didn't listen. They just poked them with their rifles and threatened to shoot them if they didn't get in the truck. The women sobbed the whole way to Plaszów, but I didn't. I was gripped by fear, but I wasn't sad to leave the ghetto. All my family were gone, and I had no more possessions of any value. There was nothing left for me there.

The truck did, after all, take us to Plaszów. It was a labor camp just a few kilometers outside Kraków. The truck stopped just outside the camp's gate, where more Jews were being unloaded from trucks. I didn't know where the others had come from: Kraków? One of the villages outside the city? Somewhere else? Some of them carried suitcases and bags; others, like us, had nothing.

"Schnell! Schnell!" a German soldier barked at me. Quickly! Quickly! He struck me in the back with the butt of his rifle, and I stumbled forward into the dirt. I scraped the skin off my palms trying to catch myself, but that was nothing compared to the screaming pain in my shoulder. I got to my feet and brushed the grit from my bleeding hands as we were herded inside.

Plaszów was a series of long, low buildings separated by dirt roads and surrounded by barbed wire. The few other men and I were separated from the women. A guard ordered us to turn over any valuables, and I gave him the few zloty I had in my pockets. After that we were ordered to take off our clothes. Reluctantly, I removed my dirty, too-short shirt and pants, and added them to a pile. Another soldier gave me a pair of wooden shoes and a blue-and-gray-striped prisoner uniform made out of a thick canvas material. I put them on and held my arms out to look at myself in my new clothes.

Now I am officially a prisoner, I thought. I almost laughed—in truth I had been a prisoner since the Nazis walled off the Kraków ghetto, but now I finally looked the part.

After we were all given uniforms, we were marched to the Plaszów tailor shop by another prisoner wearing a yellow armband. He was a *kapo*, he told us, a prisoner who'd been put in charge of other prisoners by the Nazis, so they wouldn't have to deal with us all the time. We were to do what he told us, he said, or we would feel the sting of the wooden club he carried. All of us knew enough by now to follow along and do what we were told without speaking.

There were thousands of prisoners at Plaszów, most wearing a yellow Star of David on their uniforms to show they were Jews. But there were other prisoners too, I soon learned, all of whom wore different colored triangles. The red armbands belonged to political prisoners. Green meant criminals. Black armbands were worn by gypsies, though there were very few of those, as they were usually killed straight off. Purple meant Jehovah's Witness. Homosexuals wore pink. And all of them had a little letter in their triangle to tell you where they were from: *P* meant *Polen*, or "Pole"; *T* meant *Tschechen*, or "Czech"; *J* meant *Jugoslawen*, or "Yugoslavian." There was no letter in the Jewish stars though. No matter where we had come from, we had no country. We were only Jews.

As I scanned the prisoners along the way to the tailor shop, I thought I saw a familiar face. I couldn't believe my eyes. It was Uncle Moshe!

"Uncle Moshe!" I called. "Uncle Moshe! It's me! Yanek!"

Moshe looked up, not in excitement but in horror. His eyes were wide, and he shook his head at me quickly before turning his gaze back to the ground.

"Who called there? Who was that?" our kapo barked, bringing my group to a halt. The prisoners looked back over their shoulders to show it hadn't been them, and I looked back too, as though trying to see who had called out. One of the men behind me gave me an angry glare, then turned as if to see if he could find the source of the yell behind *him*.

"The prisoners will remain silent unless spoken to," the kapo told us, and he struck a man in the back with his club. As the kapo herded us the rest of the way to the tailor shop, my face burned with shame. I was such a fool! Someone had been hurt because I'd called out to Moshe. I resolved then and there not to speak again until I could find Moshe and talk to him privately.

We worked all day in the tailor shop doing what we had done in Plaszów, only now there were more SS guards, and we were often beaten for no other reason than because we were Jews. I saw one man struck so hard in the head with a club that he fell off his stool and didn't get up again. He was dragged away and never returned, and suddenly I understood why the Plaszów tailor shop needed new workers, and always would.

That night we were marched to our barracks, where we were each given a small piece of bread and a bowl of watery soup. I was just finishing my meager meal when Uncle Moshe found me.

"Yanek!" he said. He glanced around to make sure our barrack kapo was gone, then pulled me into a hug. I hadn't hugged someone in so long that I was almost too stunned to embrace him back. Moshe held me away from him to look me over, then pulled me close again. "I'm sorry I couldn't greet you this morning, but no doubt you've seen what they do to anyone who speaks out of turn."

I nodded.

"Yanek, we haven't much time," he whispered. "Listen closely. Here at Plaszów, you must do nothing to stand out. From now on, you have no name, no personality, no family, no friends. Do you understand? Nothing to identify you, nothing to care about. Not if you want to survive. You must be anonymous to these monsters. Give your name to no one. Keep it secret, in here," Uncle Moshe said, tapping his heart with his fist.

"Are my parents here?" I asked him, daring to hope. If Moshe was alive, why not my mother and father?

Moshe shook his head. "I am sorry, boy. No. Unless they were taken to another work camp, they are most likely dead — and Plaszów is where they bring most of us from Kraków, being so close."

My legs felt wobbly. I had to sit down on my bunk, or I would have collapsed. I had known my parents might be dead — there were the rumors, after all, about where people went when they were taken. But I suppose I'd never let myself really and truly believe it until now. I didn't try to stop the tears that filled my eyes and coursed down my cheeks.

Moshe sat beside me and put a hand on my knee. "But *you* are alive, boy! There is a blessing in that. You're the only other one of us to survive."

I suddenly realized what Moshe was saying. "Aunt Gizela? Little Zytka?" I asked—his wife and daughter.

Moshe's own eyes teared up, and he quickly wiped them with the backs of his hands. "Dead," he said. "They could not work, so the Nazis shot them."

I asked about my other uncles and cousins, but Moshe shook his head. "You and I are the only ones left. You must show them you can work, boy, so you can keep living."

"I have a job in the tailor shop," I said, sniffling.

"Good. Good! Any job you can do outside the camp will help you avoid Amon Goeth."

"Who?"

"The commandant of the camp."

Outside, someone shouted.

"Roll call," Moshe said, and he stood. "We must all go and line up to be counted. Remember: You are no one. You have no name. You do not speak, you do not look at them, you do not volunteer for anything. You work, but not so hard they notice you. Gizela. Zytka.

Your parents, Oskar and Mina. They are dead and gone now, Yanek, and we would grieve for them if we could. But we have only one purpose now: *survive*. Survive at all costs, Yanek. We cannot let these monsters tear us from the pages of the world."

I nodded, wiping away my own tears, and followed Moshe to the open field in the camp where roll call was taken. We were lined up in row upon row while the Nazis checked the numbers on our uniforms against the tally on their clipboards. I realized then: They would beat us and starve us and shoot us like we didn't matter, but they would always keep track of us.

While soldiers worked their ways up and down the lines checking us off, one man in a crisp SS officer's uniform and tall riding boots walked among the prisoners, twitching a riding crop against his legs. Two sturdy-looking German shepherd dogs followed along behind him. The SS officer stopped in front of the prisoner beside me and suddenly commanded his dogs, "Attack! Attack! Kill the Jew!"

The two dogs were calm as pets one moment. In the next instant, they became rabid killers. They leaped at the man and took him down in their jaws. The man screamed for mercy and then for help as the dogs bit and tore at him right beside me. I *wanted* to help, to fight back. But Moshe glanced back at me with a warning in his eyes, and I remembered — I was no one. I had no name. They must not notice me. So I stared straight ahead at the ground, just like everyone else, silent and still as the man beside me was ripped apart. When he stopped moving and stopped crying out, the SS officer shot the man through the head with his pistol.

Goeth looked into our faces, daring one of us to react, then walked away laughing.

That was how I was introduced to Commandant Amon Goeth.

When roll call ended, Moshe went to his barrack and I went to mine. The man beside me hadn't been the only man to die at roll call — another was shot, supposedly for not smacking his cap against his leg with enough snap when doffing it for one of the soldiers. I felt as though I had survived a battle.

"What's that make the score?" I heard someone ask. It was one of the men who had already been in the camp before I arrived.

"Goeth seven, Jews nil," another man told him.

"What's that?" I asked. "How many Jews Goeth has killed since you've been here?"

"No," the man said. "How many Jews Goeth has killed today."

CHAPTER TEN

AMON GOETH WOULDN'T HAVE HIS BREAKFAST each day until he'd killed at least one Jew.

He liked most to sit on the second-floor balcony of his house overlooking the camp and shoot Jews with a rifle while he listened to music on his record player. It didn't matter who you were, or what you'd done. If you hurried through the parade grounds trying not to get shot, he would shoot at you on purpose. You had to walk through normally, acting like there wasn't a madman on the balcony above you with a rifle ready to shoot you, and hope he didn't notice you.

The best way to not get shot was to not be there in the first place.

I escaped the daily shooting gallery through my job at the tailor shop. I left early in the morning and returned in time for roll call, and then hard bread and thin soup in the barracks each night. Uncle Moshe did the same, working in a furrier's shop outside the camp. There was still a chance Goeth would get me at roll call — no one was safe, not even the kapos — but with Moshe's help, I learned to be anonymous enough to survive for months.

Then the tailor shop closed down. I was never sure why, but one morning, when the other tailors and I assembled, we were told our services at the factory were no longer required. We looked around nervously at one another. Without our off-camp job, we would be around Amon Goeth all day, and without special skills, we were even less valuable than before.

I was put to work building new barracks for the never-ceasing truckloads and trainloads of Jews brought to Plaszów every day. It was backbreaking work: digging out a level patch of earth, hauling rocks in wheelbarrows, hammering boards in place. And always there was the threat of Amon Goeth and his dogs.

After a man on my work detail was killed for moving too slowly, Uncle Moshe traded his daily rations to a kapo to get me assigned to a new job outside the camp.

I reported to my new work detail the next morning and was loaded into a truck, not knowing where we were going or what we were doing. None of us did. This was some new job no one had ever done before, and we were all a little nervous. There was always a chance that our work would be to dig graves in the woods — and then be shot to fill them.

The truck bounced to a stop, and the Nazis ordered us out. But it wasn't the woods we had been taken to, or another factory. It was the Kraków ghetto! We looked at one another in wonder — why had we been brought back to the ghetto?

A guard at the gate on Lwowska Street let us through, and we saw right away what was different: There were no more people. No one was on the streets, and no one was in the houses. The whole ghetto had been liquidated after I'd left. There was no sign of life anywhere.

"The entire ghetto must be cleaned," one of the Nazis told us. "There must be no taint of Jews left." We were told how to search each flat for anything of value, and how to sort what was left into piles on the floor for removal and disposal — clothes should be sorted in one way, household items in another.

We were to take nothing out with us, under penalty of death.

As I walked the empty streets of Podgórze, my chest felt heavy. I was overwhelmed with memories. I hadn't been gone long, and the last few years I had lived here had been a nightmare, but what I remembered wasn't the snow shoveling and the shootings and the starvation. I remembered walking to the market with my mother. Visiting my father at work. Playing ball in the street with my friends. This neighborhood had been my home once, and it always would be, even after the "taint" of Jews had been scrubbed away.

As if to tear my heart into even more pieces, I was assigned to clean out the apartment building where I had lived with my parents. While other boys worked the bottom floor, I climbed the stairs. I stopped and stood where no one could see me, remembering.

Mr. Barchwic on the second floor, singing along with the radio. Mrs. Szymansky sweeping the third-floor landing. Any minute now, I thought, my mother's voice would come calling down the stairs: "Yanek! Dinner!" I waited, but there was no radio, no sweeping, no call from my mother. Nothing but the quiet shuffling of the boys working the flats on the first floor.

I climbed the stairs to my old floor and crept down the hall. This corridor had once been so familiar to me that I had traveled it without ever really seeing it. But now it was different. Now I could see the worn spots in the hall rugs, the broken piece of molding along the ceiling, the burned-out bulb in the light fixture. There was a new smell too, something putrid, like nothing I had ever smelled before. It was strongest near the door to Mr. Tatarka's flat. The door was ajar, and I pushed it open the rest of the way to look inside.

Mr. Tatarka lay in the middle of the front room of his apartment beside the chair he'd stolen from the Immerglicks, dead in a pool of his own blood.

At least I thought it was Mr. Tatarka. The body was black and shriveled, all rags and bones and —

I stumbled back into the hall and retched. The smell, the sight of it, it was all just too much. I threw up again, tears streaming from my burning eyes, and I ran. I ran not for my old flat, the one we had shared with three other families. I ran instead for the roof, where it had just been me and my mother and father, safe and alone in our little pigeon coop. I burst through the big metal door and out onto the rooftop, gulping in big lungfuls of fresh air. The smell eventually went away, but not the memory of it — nor the vision of Mr. Tatarka's decomposing body.

I stood with my hands on my knees for a while until my breathing returned to normal, but I knew I'd have to get back soon. It wouldn't do for the Nazis to notice me for any reason. I went into the pigeon coop, fighting back all the memories of my mother and father. I sifted through what was left. Someone else had lived here after I had been taken — there was a tattered scarf I didn't remember, and a red blanket that hadn't been mine. But my father's old coat was still there in the corner. I knew I couldn't take it with me, but I picked it up and put it on, more to remember the smell of him than anything. It fit me better than it ever had, and I realized suddenly that, even though I was thin and starving, I had still grown. I was fourteen now, and almost as tall as my father had been.

I was pulling the coat off when I felt a lump in one of the sleeves. I felt it with my fingers. Something was sewn into the sleeve. Of course! Mother had sewn our extra money into our coats so it couldn't be stolen in a raid! I glanced outside the coop to make sure no one else had made it to the roof yet, and I hastily ripped the seams of my father's coat apart. There were a *thousand zloty* inside! I dug through the pile of things, found my old coat as well, and ripped out the seams. Another thousand zloty! *Two thousand zloty!* The Nazis didn't sell food in the labor camp, of course, but there were ways to buy food smuggled in from the outside. Uncle Moshe would know how!

Using a needle and thread of my mother's that had been left behind, I tore out one of the seams in my prisoner coat and sewed the money inside. I knew how to sew beautifully now from my work in the tailor shop. I finished quickly and was pleased with my work. Only the closest examination would find the money hidden inside.

I hurried to put the rest of the few things in the pigeon coop into piles, in case someone did come up here to clean up, and went back down to find the boys from my work detail. They had already made it to the top floor, and I joined in with the group cleaning out my family's old flat, carefully avoiding Mr. Tatarka's apartment.

We worked the rest of the day, putting clothes in one pile, household goods in another. I always went for the clothes first, running my hands along the seams to see if anyone else had had the same idea as my mother, and once found a pair of diamond earrings. I hooked them inside my jacket under my arms and hoped they wouldn't fall out. Uncle Moshe and I were going to eat well tonight!

All the way back to the camp, I worried I would be discovered. But the guards either didn't think we would try to sneak anything back in or figured there wasn't anything left of value in the ghetto to smuggle. For the most part they were right — more than just the people had been taken from the ghetto. Two years of imprisonment and starvation and raids had bled the ghetto dry of almost anything worth owning.

As we assembled for roll call, I whispered for Uncle Moshe to come to my barracks at dinner. I also asked him what the score was.

"Goeth nineteen, Jews nil," he whispered back. "It was a good day to get you out of the camp."

I nodded. A very good day indeed.

CHAPTER ELEVEN

UNCLE MOSHE COULDN'T BELIEVE IT WHEN I showed him the money and the earrings. He hugged me and kissed me before remembering his own warning not to let anyone else see you care about anything.

"I know a man who works in the munitions plant," Uncle Moshe whispered. "He smuggles in bread sometimes and sells it—for a price. I'll buy us a little something to eat. You've saved us, Yanek!"

Later that night, Moshe brought me half a loaf of bread—a feast! He took it out from under his shirt and gestured for me to hide it quickly.

"You mustn't let any of the other prisoners see you with it. They'll try to take it. And don't share it with anyone. Not if you want to survive, right?"

I nodded.

"The money will buy us more," Moshe whispered. "I've hidden the rest to keep it safe."

"Where?" I asked.

"I have a place no one will find."

"The kapo," someone near a window said. Someone always gave a warning when one of our overseers was coming.

"I'll see you tomorrow," Moshe said. "Remember what I told you! Don't let anyone see."

"I won't."

Uncle Moshe slipped out, and I climbed into my bunk. The bread lay against my cold skin. It wasn't warm anymore, the bread, but my heart beat faster and my mouth watered at the thought of eating it. An extra half a loaf! In Plaszów I was a rich man, which suddenly struck me as funny. Before the war, there had been loaves of bread aplenty—always one or two in the kitchen, brought back fresh from the bakery every day by my mother—and I had never thought twice about them. Now a half a loaf of bread was life itself, and my mother was gone.

The kapo did his checks to make sure everyone was in their bunks. He didn't have to worry about the man in the bunk below mine.

The man beneath me had crawled back after roll call, and hadn't moved since. He was what the others called a Muselmann. He was so thin you could count his ribs and see the bones in his arms and legs, but it wasn't just that. We were all skin and bones. Muselmanners were different in the way they breathed through their mouths, in the way they dragged their feet when they walked — if they *could* walk. Most of them just huddled on the ground on their hands and knees, even if the Germans or the kapos beat them.

But no matter how he was standing, you always knew a Muselmann from his eyes. There wasn't anything left there. Muselmanners had given up, and there was no life in their expression, no spark of a soul. They were zombies, worked and starved into a living death by our captors. If the man below me wasn't dead when they came for us tomorrow, the morning roll call would kill him.

Half a loaf of bread might have saved him, if he could even eat it. Starvation did that to you after a while. Your body got so used to not having food it got sick if you ate even half a bowl of soup. I could hear him down there, breathing his ragged breath. I could hear him dying of starvation, and I had food. Half a loaf of bread! If I just gave him part of it . . .

But Moshe had warned me: Don't share with anyone else. Not if you wanted to survive. Not if you wanted to make sure you never became a Muselmann yourself.

So I huddled on my bunk sneaking bites of bread in the dark, listening to the nameless man beneath me die.

———

My old apartment building was finished, but there were other buildings to clean in the ghetto. We worked for days, and I looked for hidden money and valuables wherever I went, but there was nothing. The place had already been picked clean before the liquidation. The Nazis had seen to that.

One night, Uncle Moshe brought me a carrot he'd bought with the money I'd found in the old coats. A whole carrot! I hadn't had a carrot since the early days in the ghetto. It was soft and mushy, but it was the most delicious thing I had ever eaten, I was sure. There was still money left, Moshe told me, lots of it. Even if I never found more money, we could keep buying a little extra food here and there for quite a while. Long enough maybe to survive. There were rumors the Russians and the Germans had abandoned their pact and were at war with each other now, making Hitler fight the English and French and Americans in the west, and the Russians in the east. One way or another, people whispered, we would be free by year's end. I couldn't believe it. Wouldn't believe it. Not until I saw an American or Russian tank rolling down the road. In the meantime, thanks to the money Moshe and I had hidden away, we would survive. No matter how long it took.

One evening when we returned to camp from cleaning the ghetto, I asked a boy in my barracks who worked inside Plaszów what the score was that day. He looked away and wouldn't answer me.

"What's wrong?" I asked him, but still he said nothing. I spun him around. "Hey! Thomas, why won't you tell me? What's the score?"

"Just one," Thomas said, looking at his feet.

"Who is it? Someone we know?"

"It was your uncle," he said at last. "The man who comes to visit you at night."

I staggered back, knocking my head on my bunk.

"No," I told him. "No, that's impossible. You're wrong. Moshe he—he doesn't work in the camp. He works at the furrier's outside Plaszów. You saw someone else."

Thomas shook his head. "They closed the furrier's and reassigned all the workers inside the camp. Your uncle was made leader of a group breaking rocks. When Goeth demanded to know how much work had been done . . ."

"What? Tell me," I demanded. My stomach was squeezing itself into a hard knot of fear.

Thomas shook his head. "Goeth didn't like his answer."

"No," I told him. "No, you're wrong. Moshe went to work today at the furrier's like always. You'll see. It was someone else."

"I'm sorry, Yanek."

"It was someone else! You'll see at roll call."

But Uncle Moshe wasn't at roll call. I searched for him where we usually met. I looked up and down the rows for him. Nothing. I wanted to call out for him, but I knew that was suicide. Moshe had taught me: Do nothing to stand out. I had to be anonymous. I had to be no one, with no name, no personality, and no family or friends to care about.

But I did care. Uncle Moshe was the last of my family. The only person I could trust in Plaszów. My only friend.

And the money I had found! Moshe had hidden it, and he had never told me where. I'd never thought to press him on it, because Moshe would always be there. We were going to survive, the two of us. We were going to survive—the last two men in the Gruener family written on the pages of the world.

Now there was only me. Yanek. I was fourteen years old, and I was alone in the world again. This time for good.

As the Nazis went through roll call I fought back my tears. If Amon Goeth saw me crying, he would kill me too.

CHAPTER TWELVE

A FEW DAYS LATER, MY JOB CLEANING THE ghetto ended, and I was put back to work in Plaszów. Without Uncle Moshe, there was no one to help me get a job outside the camp again.

The work was brutal, and the food too meager to sustain me. Some mornings I could barely get myself up out of my bunk, and I had a hard time standing at roll call. Was this how it happened? Was this how a prisoner slipped from being a person to a Muselmanner?

One night after a hard day's work digging trenches for new latrines, I collapsed to the floor of my barrack. I didn't have the strength to climb into my bunk. I was desperate to get up, but I couldn't make my legs obey me, couldn't pull up my own weight with my stick-and-straw arms. But if I didn't get up soon, the kapo would come through, and he would beat me for not being in my bunk.

No one bent to help me in my struggle to stand. Everyone else was like me — they barely had energy to spare for themselves, let alone anyone else. *Be no one, care for no one. That's how you survive.* That's what Uncle Moshe had taught me.

Moshe, I thought, my chest aching, *why aren't you here? Why did you have to die? I need help. I need a friend.*

I needed Moshe. He would have helped me back up, despite his warning not to care. Who would help me now?

I rolled myself onto my chest to push myself up, but the board beneath me was loose. Wait — a loose board?

I knew the kapo would come any minute now. But lying there on the floor and staring right at the board made me remember building the new barracks across the camp when I first arrived. There was always a space, a small one, between the wooden floor and the dirt below. If this board was loose enough —

The board pulled loose from the floor in my shaking hands. I glanced around to see if anyone had noticed, but of course no one had. The other prisoners were doing whatever they could to ignore me, just like I ignored them.

The gap in the boards would be wide enough for me to slide down inside, into the space between the floor and the ground. I was tempted to pull the board all the way up and roll down inside and disappear. But my absence from my bunk would be noticed. And what would I do, hide down there forever? I would be dead even quicker without what little bread and soup they gave us.

But tomorrow. Tomorrow after roll call, I could disappear into the barracks instead of showing up for my job. People were reassigned all the time. No one would know I was gone. I could sneak back and hide under the floor!

It was like Moshe was helping me, even though he wasn't there. He had shown me the board. As I pushed myself up off the floor with every gram of strength I had left, I felt Moshe's hand, helping me up. I reached out and grabbed hold of the bunk, clawing my way into my bed. I was not a Muselmann. Not yet.

⊷—⊶

The next morning after roll call, I grabbed the two boys I knew in my barrack, Thomas and Isaac, and showed them the board.

I don't know why I showed them. Not when you survived by looking out for yourself and only yourself. Maybe it was because I'd wanted someone to help me when I had needed it. Maybe it was just that I would be lonely in there all day. But maybe it was that I just couldn't keep the secret from someone else who could use help too. I'd done that with the black-market food Moshe had bought for us, and I'd felt guilty. I didn't want to hide out under the floor alone while everyone else was worked to death.

"We can't!" Thomas said immediately. "If we're caught, we'll be killed!"

"We'll die if we *don't* hide here," I told them. "Do you want to go back out there and be worked to death? Or worse, be killed by Goeth?"

"No! But this is begging for punishment."

"This is survival," I told them. I pulled up the board the rest of the way. "There's room inside for all three of us."

Isaac crawled down inside, and Thomas finally gave in. At first all we did was sleep. We had been worked so hard and fed so little all our bodies wanted to do was hibernate, like bears. The ground was hard, but it didn't matter. So were the wooden pallets we called beds. We slept, only waking long enough to poke one another if we snored. The sound of footsteps on the floor above woke us, and we knew it was time to come out for roll call. We couldn't miss a roll call, or they would come looking for us. As prisoners began to come back into the barracks, we pushed our way out, hurriedly replacing the floorboard and sitting down on my bunk like we had just come back from work. Nobody ever suspected—or if they did, they didn't say anything. Talking got you killed.

The more we hid under the floor, the stronger we got. We weren't healthy, not by a long shot, but without the heavy labor of the day, our bodies recovered a little. I didn't have any more trouble climbing back into my bunk each night. And Thomas, Isaac, and I started to sleep less during the day, staying awake to whisper with one another. We talked about food, mostly, but also our homes, and our families, until it hurt too much to remember. Then we'd roll over and sleep again, always listening for the soft step of prisoners' feet on the floor above to let us know when to come out.

But one day it wasn't footsteps we heard; it was voices. And in the middle of the day.

Isaac slithered over to look out the cracks in the crawl-space wall. What he saw made him gasp.

"It's Goeth!" he whispered. "Goeth and his dogs, and two guards! And they're heading for our barrack!"

"We're dead," Thomas said. "Those dogs will smell us right away. They'll find us, and we'll be shot."

The tight little crawl space under the floorboards suddenly felt like a coffin, like I was already dead and buried. My refuge from the nightmare of Plaszów was now a trap. It was all I could do not to burst out of it screaming.

"Yanek, what do we do?" Isaac asked, his voice tight with the same desperation I felt.

I looked out through the cracks. Goeth was coming closer, all shining black leather boots and crisp black uniform. One of his dogs lifted its ears and looked right at me.

I pulled back, away from the wall. "We're trapped. We have to get out of here. *We have to get out of here.*" I was almost choking on my own fear.

"And go where?" Thomas hissed. "If we leave, they'll find us in the barrack!"

"I don't care. We can't be caught here." I twisted and squirmed until I was on my back. If I could just lift that board, see the light from the room, breathe the air. It was so tight down here. So close. Closing in —

Isaac grabbed my hand. "Yanek, we can't."

"We have to!" I had to get out of this coffin. "We'll . . . we'll pretend we're on a work detail."

"He'll kill us! Goeth will kill us!" Thomas said.

"Either he'll kill us, or he won't," I told him. "But I know one thing—if he finds us hiding down here, he'll kill us for sure!"

I pushed my way up and out of the crawl space. It felt like coming up for air after being underwater. I was free of my little coffin! I gasped, filling my lungs. But if I didn't really want to die, I had to move fast. We all did. I helped Isaac out, then Thomas, and we put the board back as quickly and quietly as we could. My heart was thumping, but it made me feel alive, and feeling alive made me want to *stay* alive.

The only way we were going to get out of this was to make Goeth believe we were on a work detail, and he could smell fear as well as his dogs could. Maybe even better.

I dragged Isaac and Thomas to the door with me. "Come on," I said. "I'll do the talking."

We left the barrack right as Goeth and his dogs turned the corner.

"You there! Stop!" Goeth shouted. "Where are you going?"

My hands shook as I doffed my cap like we were

drilled to do. "We were sent to a work detail on the south side of camp, sir!" I shouted, my voice breaking I was trembling so badly.

Goeth's dogs stared at us, panting. Their ears pricked up, like they were just waiting for Goeth to tell them to attack us. Could they smell my fear? Did the dogs know I was lying?

I stood my ground and tried not to shake. I was deathly afraid, but everyone was afraid when they met Goeth, whether they'd been hiding or not.

Goeth glared at us for a long moment, then walked by without saying another word. Isaac and Thomas and I stood rooted to the spot, afraid to say or do anything that would make Goeth reconsider. When he was a few steps gone I realized that not moving *was* the wrong thing, and I grabbed my friends and pulled them along again. "Let's go," I whispered, and we hurried around the corner.

We didn't stop when Goeth was out of sight, but I could finally breathe. In trying to survive, I'd come closer than I'd ever been to dying.

I would never hide under the floorboards again.

WIELICZKA SALT MINE

1943–1944

CHAPTER THIRTEEN

ONE MORNING AT ROLL CALL, I WAS ONE OF FIFTY prisoners pulled out of the ranks and loaded onto a truck. The Nazis didn't tell us where we were going.

"They're taking us away to kill us," one of the men said.

But that didn't make any sense. Amon Goeth had no problem killing any of us at Plaszów. Why bother to load us into a truck and take us somewhere else to kill us? Just looking around at the others the Nazis had chosen, I could tell we were the strongest men at Plaszów—or at least the furthest from becoming Muselmanners. I was sure we were being taken somewhere else to work, and I was sure it had to be better than Plaszów.

My two weeks saving my strength under the floor of my barrack had saved me.

The truck pulled up outside a building with a tall spire, like a bell tower, but this was no church. The place had an industrial look to it; oil-covered motors and generators stood around it like sentinels, and train tracks led into it and out.

The Nazi in charge of our truck unloaded us, and we joined another group of prisoners who'd been brought in from somewhere else. I ended up standing next to a man who looked familiar to me, but I couldn't place him.

"Are you from Kraków?" I asked him.

"No!" he said, with surprising force. "I am no one!"

He was right, of course. I shouldn't even have asked. But I noticed two of the other men who came with me from Plaszów looking at him more intently now.

"First we will take you into the mine, to show you where you will be working," a kapo told us. "Then you will be assigned to your barracks."

We were marched into the factory, which wasn't a factory after all. It was the sheltered entrance to an enormous mine. In groups of ten and twelve we boarded elevators. I got on with the familiar-looking man and the two prisoners from Plaszów who'd been watching him. They stood close beside him now, uncomfortably close, but he didn't say anything. He just stared at the floor.

The elevator *kachunk*ed, and down, down, down, we went. Electric lights on the open elevator cage illuminated the gray-white walls of the mine shaft as we descended. Suddenly I was reminded of being under the floorboards again in Plaszów. I was squeezed in, underground. Trapped, in the dark, with death coming for me. . . .

"Salt," one of the others whispered. "The Wieliczka salt mine. It has to be."

My trance was broken. I reached out my hand to touch the wall and tasted my fingers. It was true — the walls were made of salt!

The elevator car hit bottom, and we were guided through a labyrinth of tunnels and small chambers.

"You'll be working room forty-seven," our kapo told us. "Level seven."

We marched down salt stairs, we crawled along salt floors, we passed stalagmites formed from salt water dripping off the ceiling. I had never seen anything like it. The mine was like a strange dreamworld. Very soon we left the electric lights behind and could see only as far ahead of us as our kapo's carbide headlamp.

"Maybe you're thinking it would be easy to slip away in the tunnels," our kapo told us. "Maybe you are thinking it would be easy to escape into the darkness. There are nine levels. Three hundred kilometers of tunnels. Maybe you are thinking we would never find you."

The kapo stopped and turned his headlamp on us.

"You're right. We *wouldn't* find you. You would be lost forever in a maze blacker than night, with nothing to eat but salt, and nothing to drink but salt water. If I were you, I wouldn't get lost — either on purpose, or by accident."

We all followed closer behind him the rest of the way.

The kapo showed us the room where we would be working. The picks and shovels we would be using. The carts we would fill with them. The other prisoners who worked the mine were already back in their barracks, asleep. We would get up with them before dawn and come right back here to work, without a full night's sleep. Just the thought of it made my arms and legs ache.

The kapo took us out a different way, through a vast chamber where every footstep echoed. One of the men in front of me stumbled, and a piece of salt clattered off the wooden boardwalk beneath us and splashed. Water! There was an entire lake under here. It rippled and glimmered black in the light from the kapo's lamp.

Up more steps we went, and another elevator, until we came to another huge chamber, this one lit with electric light again. Here there was no lake, but something even more amazing: statues! Dozens of figures, all carved out of salt. And the lights in the ceiling—they were chandeliers. Chandeliers made out of salt. After so many months and years of dirty streets and peeling paint, of gray uniforms and spartan barracks, it was astounding that there could still be beauty in the world. Especially here, a mile underground.

"The workers, the miners—they did this," whispered the man who'd told me the name of the mine before. "Some of these statues are a thousand years old."

There were trolls and serpents and gnomes. There were Polish knights and kings and queens. I wished they could somehow, magically, come to life and free us—save us.

They stayed still though, frozen in salt. As trapped and helpless as we were.

The last room was another monument left by former miners in Wieliczka's happier past. It was a temple, a chapel—no, an underground cathedral. There were more statues, an altar, a rail. Everything a Catholic needed to hold services. But praying hadn't done the miners any good either. The Nazis owned almost all of Poland now, even three hundred meters underground.

Night had fallen and the stars were out when we got back topside. We were taken to our barracks, which were no better than our last at Plaszów. Because we'd missed dinner we were sent to bed without any food. We knew better than to complain, and most of us went to our beds as quickly as we could. Morning, as we all knew, would be there before any of us were ready for it.

But the two men who'd been looking strangely at the man I thought was familiar cornered him once the kapo was gone.

"Your name is Holtzman, isn't it?" one of them said.

"No," the familiar-looking man said. "No, my name is Finkelstein!"

"You were in Kraków, weren't you?" the other man said. "You were one of the Judenrat's policemen."

Of course! That's why I remembered him! How could I have forgotten that face? He was the man who had brought the Nazis to my flat, the one who had stolen everything else from us while the Nazi took my mother's ring. I remembered my mother's eyes that day, the emptiness that had never completely gone away. I'd been so scared, so protective, that I hadn't even felt anger.

I did now.

"No!" the policeman said. There was panic in his eyes. "My name is Finkelstein! From Zielonki!"

"Quiet in there!" a kapo's voice shouted from outside. The two men said nothing more to the policeman, but they watched him all the way back to their bunks. That night, I could hear the man crying softly in his bed, until someone hissed at him to shut up.

———

The morning was cold, with only lukewarm, coffee-flavored water to fight off the chill. It was colder still underground, where it was always damp and the sun never shone. The low ceiling made us all walk like old crones, and I noticed that even when they could, some of the old-timers never stood up straight anymore. Their backs were permanently bent.

I was given my own carbide light, my own pickax, and my own place to work. It was heavy work, and boring; there was nothing to it but swinging my pickax again and again, breaking off big chunks of salt that another prisoner shoveled into a donkey cart. I chipped away, my arms already starting to ache from weakness and malnutrition, when I heard someone cry out from the chamber around the corner from mine.

"What's this? How did this happen? Who's done this?"

It was the voice of one of the kapos. It wasn't said in the tone the kapos used to taunt us or goad us into working harder. This was something different. Something confused. Something scared. The other kapos heard it in his voice right away and ran around the corner to help. Without guards, we put down our picks and our shovels and hurried to peek around the corner behind them.

It was the Judenrat policeman. Holtzman or Finkelstein or whatever his name was. His head had been smashed in with a shovel, and the rest of his body was gashed and torn and bleeding. In the carbide light from a dozen watching headlamps, something glittered and shone in his cuts.

Salt. Someone had rubbed salt in all his wounds. Like Abimelech, in the book of Judges, who sowed the fields of his own people with salt after he put down their rebellion. I remembered reading about him while studying the Torah with my father, long before the war.

This was punishment and purification, all in one.

"I said I want to know who did this!" the kapo yelled.

I looked around from face to face, trying to see who had done it. The men who had accused him in the barracks weren't there. It could have been any of them. It could have been all of them.

No one said anything, and I worried we would all be whipped for the crime. But the kapo only shook his head.

"What do I care if you kill one another? You'll all be dead soon enough anyhow. You. And you," he said, pointing to two of the prisoners watching nearby. "Drag his body out of here, weight him down, and dump him in the underground lake."

No one said another word about him. The kapos sent us back to our places, and I chipped away at the salt wall again until they told me to stop.

That night, I dreamed the salt statues came to life and set on our captors with their swords, but every one of the statues had the face of the dead man.

TRZEBINIA
CONCENTRATION CAMP

1944

CHAPTER FOURTEEN

OUR JOB WAS TO MOVE A PILE OF ROCKS.

They were big rocks, and it was a big pile. The rocks were heavy and rough, and we were given no wheelbarrows or gloves. The rocks had to be moved from one side of the assembly field to another, and the Nazis yelled at us and beat us if we were too slow or if they thought we were carrying a rock that was too small for us. I put my arms around another stone and lifted, my back crying out in pain. The rock tore and scraped at my skin as I cradled it to my chest and staggered across the yard to dump it in the new pile. Then I did it again. And again. One of the other men stumbled and collapsed, and the guards fell on him with sticks and clubs. I hefted another rock and kept working while I tried not to let the Nazis see how afraid I was. They were like Amon Goeth's dogs — they could smell fear on you, and they liked nothing better than to attack when you were at your weakest.

By midday, my arms and hands and chest were so raw and bruised I couldn't have gone on, but by then we were finished. I would have dropped to the ground but I knew I would just be beaten for it, so I stood with the others, wobbling on my shaking legs while I waited for the guards to tell us what new task awaited us.

"Good," the SS officer in charge of us said. "Now move it back."

I blinked stupidly, not understanding at first. We had just worked all morning to move this pile of stones across the camp, and now the Nazis were changing their minds? The other prisoners and I looked at one another to see if we had heard right.

"I said move this pile back to where it was!" the SS officer yelled. He moved through our group, hitting us with a stick until we moved. "You will move it to where it was, and then you will move it again! Now work!"

Such was life at the Trzebinia concentration camp.

I had been transferred there after a short time mining salt at Wieliczka. Wieliczka had been hard, but Trzebinia was worse, because at Trzebinia the Nazis played games. The Nazis were making us work just to work. This was all a game to them, like a hand of cards or a soccer match. We were the ball, to be kicked around for their sport.

My arms shook as I picked up the same stone that I had just carried across the compound, but not from weariness this time. From fury. I fumed as I hefted the stone and trudged back across the muddy compound. But they wanted me to be angry. They wanted me to say something, or frown, or mumble curses at them. They were watching me for it. Watching all of us. Like schoolyard bullies, they wanted to provoke us, and then they would beat us as punishment.

At Trzebinia I worked all day moving piles of rocks back and forth, digging holes six feet deep and then filling them back in again. I ate watery broth and week-old bread once a night and passed out on a wooden pallet with no mattresses or pillows or blankets. I was an animal to them, a pack mule. But beasts were never treated so poorly. Working animals were expensive. They had value. I was a Jew. We were lower than animals. They could kill as many of us as they wanted, and there would always be another trainload of us to take our place.

But as angry as I was at the Nazis, I was even angrier at my fellow prisoners. How could we take this abuse so quietly, so meekly, with our heads bowed and a quick tip of the cap to our killers? Yes, the Nazis had clubs and guns, but there were far more of us than there were of them. If we turned on them all at once, we could overcome them. We were not animals to be led to the slaughter! We were thinking, feeling human beings! One day, in the middle of hauling rocks again, I vowed not to be killed without a fight. My father, Uncle Moshe, the Jewish elders, they were all wrong. We shouldn't be trying to survive, we should be trying to *win*. Instead of waiting for the British or the Americans or the Russians to save us, we should be saving ourselves.

I'm not going to let them line me up on the edge of a pit and shoot me, I told myself. *I will fight back. I will kick the Nazis in the shins. I will run. I won't go like a sheep to the slaughter!*

At roll call that night, someone else had the same thought. One of the Nazis struck him with a club, but instead of taking the beating meekly the prisoner raised his arms and grabbed the stick. He wrestled it from the shocked officer's hands and struck him with it in the head, knocking his Nazi hat into the muck, striking his raised arms again and again.

Yes! Yes, I thought. *It begins here. Together we can take them all!* I looked around anxiously to see if anyone else felt as I did, if anyone else would take up the charge, but everyone had their heads down. No! This was our chance! If we fought together—

Crack! I jumped at the sound. With the fiery spark of a pistol, it was all over. The prisoner who had fought back crumpled to the ground, dead from a bullet to the brain, and the assaulted officer was hurried away from the assembly grounds. The camp's soldiers appeared in force around the edges of our lines, pointing rifles at us, and the camp commandant hurried out from his cozy office. When he heard the report from his officers, he turned on the prisoners.

"You!" he cried, pointing at a boy who had been standing right next to the man who fought back. "You were a part of this plot to escape!"

"W-what?" the boy stammered. He wasn't much older than me. "No! No, I didn't even know him!"

Guards grabbed the boy and dragged him to the front of our lines, where the Nazis had built a gallows for hanging prisoners.

"And this man," the commandant said, pointing into the crowd. "And this one. And him. And him. And him."

He was picking people at random now in his fury, punishing innocent people for the dead man's effrontery. I shrank back. I recognized the boy and two of the other men from my barrack. Like me, they couldn't even have known who the dead man was.

"I'm innocent!" the boy my age sobbed as they dragged him up onto the gallows and put the hangman's noose around his neck. "I never tried to escape! I promise! I've done everything you asked!"

I shook with helplessness and rage, but also with fear. This is what fighting back earned you. More abuse. More death. Half a dozen Jews would be murdered today because one man refused to die without a fight. To fight back was to die quickly and to take others with you.

This was why prisoners went meekly to their deaths. I had been so resolved to fight back, but I knew then that I wouldn't. To suffer quietly hurt only you. To suffer loudly, violently, angrily—to fight back—was to bring hurt and pain and death to others.

"Please!" the boy cried. "I never tried to escape. I'm innocent!" He looked out on all of us, those of us with the courage to look up from the ground. "Remember," he begged us. "I did nothing."

The hangman kicked the chair out from under him, and the boy's body jerked as his neck was broken.

I kept my head held high and watched, vowing never to forget.

CHAPTER FIFTEEN

MY WORK DETAIL WAS ON ITS WAY TO THE quarry to break more rocks one morning when another kapo came to speak to ours. The two kapos talked for a moment, and our kapo ordered us to stop. I kept my head down, but tried to look around with my eyes to see what was going on. Something different was happening, and different was never good. Our kapo kept us standing there without saying anything else for a long time. What was happening? Why had we stopped? Were we in trouble? Were we going to be killed? The other prisoners had to be asking themselves the same questions, but of course none of us spoke. To speak was to invite a beating. We would be told our fates when our captors decided we needed to know.

"Turn around," our kapo said at last. "March."

We headed away from the quarry, which would have been a relief if I thought we were going someplace better. We passed a place where prisoners were shot over the pits they had dug for themselves, and I said a silent prayer of thanks. But then we passed the barracks, and the main gate. We were being marched to the depot. A train waited at the side rail, but it didn't have passenger cars. It was fitted out with cattle cars. We were to be transported like livestock.

We were herded up a ramp into one of the train cars under the whips and clubs of the kapos and SS officers. I was one of the first ones inside. The car was empty and looked recently washed, but it smelled of urine and vomit and excrement. I reeled back, but there was nowhere to go.

"In! In!" the guards yelled at us, and I was pushed up against the far wall. More and more prisoners were forced into the car. They packed so many of us in I was crushed between three other men and the wall, but it was like that for everyone. I couldn't even raise my arm. I felt trapped again, like I had felt under the floorboards and down in the salt mine. I couldn't be here. I had to have space. Air.

"I can't breathe. I can't breathe!" a man at the other end of the car started to scream, giving voice to my panic. "Let me out! I need to get out of here!" He kicked at the wall of the cattle car. "Please! I can't take it!"

Crack! An SS officer shot the man through the wall of the cattle car, and he no longer had to worry about not being able to breathe. If I panicked, if I broke, I would suffer the same fate. Instead I worked my way toward a ventilation grate on the wall of the train car and pressed my face up against it, breathing in the fresh air from outside. My heart still raced, but at least I could breathe.

We stood squeezed into the train car for half a day while the Nazis loaded more prisoners into other cars. We had no food, no water, and no way to go to the bathroom. Soon I understood why the train car had smelled so bad, and would only smell worse before this ordeal was through.

Late in the afternoon the train lurched and we were away. None of us knew where we were going. I hoped it would be better than Trzebinia, but by now I knew not to dream. False hope only made things worse.

It was cold along the wall of the cattle car. Wind whipped through the spaces in between the car's wooden slats, making me shiver. But at least I had air. The prisoners in the middle complained of it being too hot and too close, and of not being able to breathe. So I shivered while I sucked the freezing air into my lungs, and I didn't complain.

As the train made its way to wherever we were going, I watched the landscape slide by. Plaszów, Wieliczka, Trzebinia — they had all been right around Kraków, my home. Now I was truly leaving home and seeing the outside world for the first time. I had never imagined it would be under these circumstances.

I saw snow-covered fields. Farmhouses with electric lights burning in the windows. Forests. A river. A busy road with cars and trucks. After all my time in the work camps, it was strange to see people in the real world, eating dinner and going to school and watching movies. But that was the world for non-Jews. My world was concentration camps and salt mines, starvation and cattle cars.

The train slowed, and the other prisoners began to stir. Were we at our final destination? Did anyone recognize where we were? I watched through the grate as a little train station slid into view, but I couldn't make out the name on the station sign. I could see people though, regular people.

Polish men carrying briefcases. Polish women pushing strollers. A child in a blue coat pointed at our train, and her mother turned her away. Two boys waited with their parents beside a stack of luggage. They were going on a trip. Maybe on vacation. "They're going to turn you into soap, Jews!" one of the boys yelled. He couldn't have been much older than five or six.

"No," his older brother said. "They're taking you to the gas chambers!" The boys scooped up snow from the platform and threw snowballs at the train. One of them exploded on the grate near me, and I was showered with slush and ice. I was angry until I realized the snow was water, and that I was dying of thirst. I licked what I could off my face and my shirt.

The train lurched and we were off again, the boys taunting us and throwing more snowballs at us as we left.

"And you wanted to escape," a man near me whispered to another man. "You wanted to run off into the woods and fight. But do you see? Do you see what the rest of them think about us? These people would sell you back to the Nazis for a sack of potatoes and then toast you at the dinner table."

We did not arrive at our destination that night. Nor the entire next day. And still we had no food or water. I drifted in and out of sleep, that blessed escape from hunger. I would have collapsed from exhaustion if I hadn't been held up by the prisoners squeezed in around me.

One morning or night—I couldn't tell which it was—I woke up to find the man next to me leaning heavily on my shoulder. I shook him to wake him up, but he wouldn't open his eyes. Something about the way he stood there, something about the way he moved, stiff and awkward, made my skin prickle. His flesh was gray, like a Muselmann's, his lips cracked and frozen at the corners. Then I realized: He wasn't breathing.

The man leaning on me was dead.

I squirmed and twisted, trying to push him away, but there was nowhere for either of us to go. The men near me roused from their sleep to grumble at me to be still, and I gave up. The dead man would be my companion until we got to wherever it was we were going. I worried I wouldn't be able to sleep again, knowing there was a corpse leaning on me, but soon the cold took me and I reentered the half-awake world of the barely alive.

I woke again to an orange horizon. A sunrise? A sunset? My throat was cold and dry, my tongue like burlap. It had snowed while I was asleep, and the ventilation grate near me was covered with the stuff — grayish white from the engine's smoke. I tried to reach it with my tongue, to lick some of that precious frozen water off the grate, but it was just out of reach. My arms were pinned at my sides by the crush of people in the car, but I wanted that snow. I needed that snow to survive. Slowly, painfully, I pulled my arm up between the dead man and the sleeping one beside us. The sleeper muttered in his sleep as I jostled him, and he pushed my hand back down without even waking. But I had to have that snow. I pushed again, and again the man pushed back. I elbowed him in his sunken stomach. He whimpered in his sleep and stopped fighting. My arm was free!

I scooped snow from the grate. My thin fingers were so cold they were blue, but I didn't care. I shoved the snow in my mouth like a toddler eating cake. My throat was so dry I gagged on it, but I forced the melting snow down, ignoring the shocking pain in my teeth from the cold. It was water, wonderful water! Not even a pastry at the corner bakery on Lwowska

Street had ever tasted so good. With a pang I remembered going there on Thursdays with my father, eating a treat and watching the pigeons in the park while my father read his newspaper. I pushed the memory away and reached for more gray snow.

The orange horizon turned out to be a sunrise, which turned into a bright blue winter morning. Our train slowed again, this time not for a station. We were shunted to a side track while another train of cattle cars passed us, going in the opposite direction. The other train slowed, then stopped alongside.

"You there," someone called from across the way. "You there, in the other train."

I squinted through the slats in the wall. There were people in the other train, packed in like us. We were all Jews being shipped around occupied Poland like coal or meat.

"What?" a man a meter or two away from me answered.

"What does our train say? Where are we going?" the man in the other train asked.

I hadn't thought the trains would have our destination on them, but most trains did, I remembered. There were plates at the top that could be switched out for different destinations. I peered through the slats at the other car, trying to see.

"Treblinka," I called, seeing the placard at last. "It says you're going to Treblinka." I didn't know the place. "Where are we going?"

"Birkenau," the man in the other train called. I had never heard of Birkenau either, but the word spread through the train in scared whispers. *Birkenau. Birkenau. Birkenau.*

The other train rocked and started moving again, and soon we too were on our way.

The man next to me, the live one, mumbled and shook his head.

"What is it?" I asked. "What's Birkenau? Another work camp?"

"You don't go to Birkenau to work," the man said, his voice hoarse and dry. "You go there to die. Birkenau isn't a concentration camp. It's a death camp."

A chill ran through me. The boys at the depot had been right, I realized. They had known. The Nazis were going to kill us. They were going to turn us into soap. The train rocked back and forth, back and forth. Outside, it began to snow again.

"You want my advice?" the man next to me rasped.

"When they take us to the gas chambers, try to stand right under the exhaust vents."

"Is that how you survive?"

The man laughed, or tried to. "No. You won't survive. None of us will. But if you stand under the exhaust vents, you won't suffer as long before you die."

BIRKENAU
CONCENTRATION CAMP
1944–1945

CHAPTER SIXTEEN

THE TRAIN ARRIVED AT BIRKENAU AT NIGHT.
The cars clanked and groaned as the train came to a
stop half a kilometer outside the gates. It was a cloudy
night, and should have been dark, but the sky was lit
up red like a bonfire. Black chimneys stood up in sil-
houette against the glowing sky, shooting flames from
their tops, and the smell of burning flesh filled the air.
I gagged.

I waited for the train to move again, to take us into
that awful factory, but we didn't move. We sat for what
must have been hours, all of us who could see out
watching the flames, knowing that was where we were
going. Why were they holding us here? Was this one
last torture, one last joke? Did they want to drive us to

panic? To madness? If they did, it was working. The longer we waited, the more anxious I got. What was going on? Why weren't we moving?

"What are they waiting for?" I said at last, my voice hoarse from thirst and fear.

"Don't you see the fires in the chimneys?" a man next to me said. "They have to finish off the last train-load before they have room for us."

I took in his words, too weak to react. We were just another raw material, waiting to be processed. Shovel us in, shovel us out.

I dozed again. Every time I woke, I was still in the cold train car, a dead man leaning against me. At last, the train jolted and began to move, and I woke for good to a pale yellow sun rising above the trees in the distance. They were taking us inside to the furnaces. They were taking us inside to die.

The train-car door opened. For a few steps the dead body next to me came with us, held up between the living as we pushed for the door. But soon there was more space, and he fell, slumping to the floor with the others who had died on the trip. There were dozens of them, rag-and-bone skeletons who had perished of hunger, or thirst, or the cold, or suffocation, or overwork. We climbed over them, gulping in the fresh air outside before the kapos and soldiers whipped us and shouted at us to line up.

We assembled in a field just beyond the train cars, those of us who survived, looking more dead than alive. After another roll call to see which of us were still alive, the Nazis marched us toward one of the big brick buildings with chimneys.

So this was it. The reality began to sink in, and I slumped under its weight. They really were going to kill us. I had come so far, endured so much agony and suffering.

I had survived the work gangs in the ghetto. Baked bread under cover of night. Hidden in a pigeon coop. Had a midnight bar mitzvah in the basement of an abandoned building. I had watched my parents be taken away to their deaths, had avoided Amon Goeth and his dogs, had survived the salt mines of Wieliczka and the sick games of Trzebinia. I had done so much to *live*, and now, here, the Nazis were going to take all that away with their furnace!

I started to cry, the first tears I had shed since Moshe had died. Why had I worked so hard to survive if it was always going to end like this? If I had known, I wouldn't have bothered. I would have let them kill me back in the ghetto. It would have been easier that way. All that I had done was for nothing.

In a large empty room we were ordered to undress and pile our striped uniforms in a corner. In a different corner was another stack of clothes — silks of bright red and blue and purple and green. Gypsy clothes. Now we knew who had fed the fires of Birkenau while we waited our turn outside. I was still crying as I pulled my shirt off and added it to the pile. The tears came unbidden, but I didn't try to stop them. Some of the other men were crying. Most weren't. I didn't care. I was tired. Tired of fighting. Tired of being brave. Tired of surviving.

They whipped us and beat us again to herd us into the next room, where showerheads lined the ceiling. I remembered what the man on the train had said, that you died fastest if you stood underneath one of the showerheads, where the gas came out. Instead I moved away from them, near one of the stone columns set throughout the room.

They packed us in again, just like on the train, but there was still a little room to move. When the door clanked shut, some of the men cried out. By now we all knew why we were here, and what they were going to do to us. Some people panicked and beat on the door, yelling for the Nazis to let us out, to have mercy, to spare us. Some people cursed them. Some people closed their eyes and muttered prayers. Some just stared off into space, waiting to die.

Tears streamed down my face, tears I didn't know I had left, and I slid down the column to the ground, burying my head in my hands. Mother, Father, my aunts and uncles, my cousins, my friends in Kraków, I missed them all so much.

We waited, but no gas came. The cries of the men grew louder and more desperate. I stayed frozen to where I sat, not knowing what to think. Why were they waiting now? Maybe someone was standing on the hose, I thought crazily, and I started to giggle. Yes. That was it. Or maybe they couldn't get the fire for the furnace going. Maybe the match kept blowing out. Or the kindling wouldn't catch fire. I laughed out loud at that, and a prisoner standing over me looked down at me like I was insane. Maybe I was. The Nazis had finally broken me. It was all a big joke. I could see that now. There was no rhyme or reason to whether we lived or died. One day it might be the man next to you at roll call who is torn apart by dogs. The next day it might be you who is shot through the head. You could play the game perfectly and still lose, so why bother playing at all?

Still the gas didn't come. I pulled myself to my feet and pushed my way through the men until I was standing right underneath one of the showerheads.

"Go on!" I yelled at the showerhead. "Go on, do it! I dare you!" I laughed again. "What are you waiting for?" I cried. "Kill me! I give up! You win!"

The pipes rattled and moaned. Something was finally coming out. The men in the room got quiet, like we were all holding our breaths, and I reached my arms up toward the ceiling.

Kill me, I prayed. *Please kill me and put an end to this. I'm ready.*

Water rained down on me. Freezing water so cold it made me scream. Water! Not gas! I was going to live! I laughed and cried, and so did the other men. We celebrated as we shivered, hugging one another and shaking hands, all of us granted a last-minute reprieve by the Nazis.

I was alive.

CHAPTER SEVENTEEN

AFTER THE SHOWER, NOTHING SEEMED TO MAT-
ter as much to me. I knew it was a game to the
Nazis — kill us, don't kill us, to them it didn't really
matter — but even so, I was glad I had made it through.

I had been ready to die. But when water came out of
those showers, not gas, it was like I was born again. I
had survived, and I would keep surviving.

I was alive.

The Nazis lined us up, still naked and shivering.
First they shaved our heads. With our hair gone, we all
looked alike — young and old. Next they marched us
to a different room, where soldiers waited at tables
with what looked like big oversized pencils with wires
attached to them. As we worked our way toward

them, person after person, I could hear screams of pain ahead of us. I had no idea what they were doing to us, but they weren't killing us. That was all that mattered, I told myself. I could handle pain.

By the time I got to the head of the line, I understood what was happening. We were being tattooed. I watched as the man ahead of me had letters and numbers carved into his skin in black ink with an electric needle. When it was my turn, the Nazi with the tattoo pencil grabbed my arm and started to write. The pain was awful as he dragged the vibrating needle over my skin, but I knew better than to cry out or beg him to stop. Besides, nothing could be worse than what had already happened to me. I had been in a gas chamber. I had looked up into a showerhead and waited for death to come, and it had passed me by. I was *alive*. A tattoo was nothing to me. Not in that moment.

B-3087.

That's what the Nazis carved into my skin. *B* for *Birkenau*, *3087* for my prisoner number. That was the mark they put on me, a mark I would have for as long as I lived. B-3087. That was who I was to them. Not Yanek Gruener, son of Oskar and Mina. Not Yanek Gruener of 20 Krakusa Street, Podgórze, Kraków.

Not Yanek Gruener who loved books and science and American movies.

I was Prisoner B-3087.

But I was *alive*.

After the room where we were tattooed, we were taken to another room with a huge pile of old, used prisoner uniforms, and told to find something that fit. The soldiers made us run, beating us with clubs if we took too long to find new pants and a shirt, so we took whatever we could as fast as we could. I ended up with pants that were too short and a shirt that was too big, but I was lucky to get a pair of wooden shoes that fit. That was important. Shoes were everything in the camps. I moved fast and wasn't beaten. I could play the game as well as anybody. I had made it this far, hadn't I? I was alive.

When we were showered and tattooed and dressed again, we were taken to our new barracks. They were worse than any barracks I'd seen yet. The ground at Birkenau was like a swamp, wet and thick with mud, and there were no floors in the barracks. There was no heat or electric light either. The bunks weren't beds but shelves, stacked three tall on top of one another, and they stuffed us in again as they had on the trains. There were no mattresses, no pillows, no blankets. Just old, wet straw, when there was anything at all. There were so many of us we could only all lie one direction or we couldn't lie down at all. It didn't matter. I was alive. I couldn't help thinking it over and over again.

I felt something at my feet, deep inside the shelf, and I reached down to get it. It was a scrap of colorful cloth, a bandanna or a handkerchief, probably left there by one of the gypsies who'd slept in these bunks before us. I tucked the scrap up under my head, hoping to use it as a bit of pillow against my ear, but there was something hard inside it. I unknotted the cloth and found an object hidden within: a little wooden horse. It was a simple children's toy, a rough carving that just hinted at four legs and a head, but it was smooth and dark like it had been played with. Some gypsy boy or girl had loved this horse. Had somehow kept it with them always, right up until the very end. Had they known they were going to die? Had they left their little horse behind so it wouldn't die with them? So some part of them might survive and be remembered?

"We have a boy who is thirteen today," a man on my shelf said. I raised my head, as did one or two others. "Who will stand with him?"

No one stirred.

"Are there not ten men here who will make a minyan with us?"

"Be quiet," someone told him. "Go to sleep."

"How can you care about such things in a place like this?" someone else asked.

"It is even more important here and now," the man said.

Someone scoffed. "Tomorrow he will be dead. We all will. None of it matters anymore."

I was tired, and starving, and my arm burned from the tattoo. But suddenly I thought standing in a minyan for somebody's bar mitzvah was the most important thing in the word. Worth losing sleep over. Worth being punished or killed.

"I'll do it," I said. The men around me were quiet for a minute after I spoke, and then someone else said yes. And another. And another. When there were ten of us, we climbed down onto the muddy floor, and the man who had first spoken began to pray. More men came down then, more than ten, until we filled the whole ground. The boy looked so young, but I knew I could be only one or two years older than he was. With a start, I realized I had probably missed my own birthday. I was fifteen now, maybe even sixteen. It was winter, but I had no idea what month it was, let alone what day. I had been in concentration camps for more than two years. I looked at the boy and remembered my own hasty bar mitzvah in Kraków. I had been so young then, a lifetime ago.

The ceremony was fast so we wouldn't be caught. When it was over, the men all whispered "Mazel tov" and climbed back onto their shelves. I went up to the boy and pressed the wooden horse into his hands, the only present I could give him. The boy looked at me with big, round eyes. Had I ever been so young?

"We are alive," I told him. "We are alive, and that is all that matters. We cannot let them tear us from the pages of the world."

I said it as much for me as for him. I said it in memory of Uncle Moshe, and my mother and father, and my aunts and other uncles and cousins. The Nazis had put me in a gas chamber. I had thought I was dead, but I was alive. I was a new man that day, just like the bar mitzvah boy. I was a new man, and I was going to *survive*.

CHAPTER EIGHTEEN

I STOOD AT THE WATER PUMP, SCRUBBING MY body. It was bitterly cold out, but I didn't care. I would scrub my body, I decided, each and every morning, no matter how cold it was, no matter how tired I was. I was alive, and I meant to stay that way.

We had no soap, but at least I was able to wash away the caking dirt of Birkenau. I paid careful attention to where I had been tattooed. Too many others had let their tattoos get infected, and that had taken them to the camp surgeon. You didn't want to go to the camp surgeon. Ever. I even rubbed my teeth with my wet fingers — we had no toothbrushes or toothpaste, of course, but it felt important to remember what it was like to be human.

As I scrubbed the taint of Birkenau from my body, I read the signs the Nazis had posted above the water pump: THE BLOCK IS YOUR HOME: MAINTAIN CLEANLINESS! and ONE LOUSE—YOUR DEATH! Big jokers, the Nazis. You could play by the rules, keep yourself clean, do everything right, and still the Nazis would kill you for looking at them wrong. But I played the game.

Work at Birkenau was as bad as everywhere else. Here, as in Plaszów, we were to build new barracks. The ground for the new section was so big it would double the size of the camp when it was finished. The Nazis called the new camp B III, but we prisoners called it Mexico. I don't know where the name started, but Mexico always sounded exotic to me. Warm and sunny, with beaches and laughing faces. Maybe that's why the prisoners nicknamed it Mexico. To make them think of something very different from what B III really was. The camp storehouse, where the Nazis kept all the valuables the Jews from towns and villages brought with them when they first arrived, we called Canada. Food was weak coffee substitute in the morning, watery soup at lunch, and bread at night. The bread was hard and tasteless and had to serve as breakfast as well. The soup was tepid, and you were lucky if there was a limp potato floating in it. I learned a trick with the soup, which was to wait awhile before lining up for it. The heavier parts of the soup sank to the bottom. If you were among the last in line, your soup was thicker. I almost always got some chunk in my soup by holding back until the end. Just that little bit of extra food might keep me from becoming a Muselmann.

We were forbidden to go out at night, so instead of the camp latrines we had to use a barrel in the barrack if we had to go to the bathroom. There were two barrels for five hundred people, so we learned to go to the latrines during the day as much as we could. There was one latrine per prison block — really just a row of holes cut in boards that sat over the cesspit. Prisoners stood guard at the door with clocks. Their job was to make sure no prisoner spent more than two minutes in the latrine. If you took longer than that, an SS guard would go in and beat you with a club until you left. There was to be no dawdling at Birkenau.

The joke was on the Germans this time though. By leaving the same prisoners stationed at the latrine, the one place we all had to go throughout the day, they gave us secret postmen. The Nazis never wanted us to talk to one another, but if ever you had a message for someone else, you could whisper it to the prisoner on watch at the latrine door as you went in. He would remember it, and quietly whisper it to the recipient when he came to take care of his business later that day.

One day as I went into the latrine with another prisoner, I heard the watchman whisper, "Tonight." I didn't know what the message meant, but it wasn't for me anyway.

That night I was fast asleep on my shelf, slotted in with all the other prisoners in my barrack, when shouts startled me out of my sleep. Kapos and SS guards were in the barracks, yelling at us to get up and smacking at prisoners with their clubs. I blinked, disoriented and scared, but I managed to tumble off of my shelf. This was something new for Birkenau, where usually they let us at least sleep through the night.

We quickly assembled in the yard, standing in rows, and I could tell immediately that something was wrong. The floodlights in the towers weren't sliding lazily over the grounds like usual. They were turned outside, where they swept the woods quickly, back and forth. Guard dogs barked beyond the barbed-wire fence surrounding the camp, and cars and tanks rolled by outside.

"Prison break," a man next to me whispered.

A prison break! Who? How? My heart thumped in my chest. I wished I was with them, whoever they were, running for the forest, the hills — anywhere but here.

Get out, I prayed for them. *Get away. Fly.*

A Nazi came around, checking our numbers against a clipboard. There were always prisoners who couldn't get out of bed again, who had become Muselmanners. That's what the Nazis wanted, anyway, to kill us with work and starvation. But which of the missing prisoners were dying back in the barracks, and which of them were running free in the woods?

The Nazi grabbed my hand and read the number on my arm, then moved on to the next prisoner. My wrist still hurt where he'd grabbed me, his grip was so tight. The Nazis were mad. Prisoners weren't supposed to stand up for themselves. Prisoners weren't supposed to escape.

Will they make it out? Where will they go if they do? Could I escape from Birkenau too? I wondered. Could

I live in the woods eating berries and nuts, sleeping out in the cold? It couldn't be worse than the camps, and maybe not every Pole was like the awful boys throwing snowballs at the train station. Maybe some sympathetic Pole would take me in, hide me in their barn.

We stood for hours, late into the night. They even went through the roll call again, as though some of us might have slipped off in between, which didn't seem possible. Then, almost at dawn, there were shouts of excitement from the Nazis beyond the fence. The gates were opened, and a ragged bunch of prisoners were marched back inside, all beaten and bloodied. I immediately felt sick to my stomach and swayed on my feet.

The escaped prisoners hadn't made it. They'd been caught. How, I didn't know, and how many had run and how many they'd caught I didn't know either. But these men hadn't made it, and the price would be severe.

The SS officer of the watch sneered at us. "There is no escape from Birkenau!" he cried. "No escape! Perhaps some of you are thinking about running. There is no one waiting to help you on the outside. There is nowhere for you to hide. You will be caught! And here is what we do to those who try to escape!"

They lined the men up against a wall in the assembly yard. *Rat-tat-tat-tat!* The watch officer gunned them down himself, riddling their bodies with bullets.

"Bring forward their work detail!" the guard cried. Other men were pulled out of the ranks — prisoners who had done nothing but work alongside the men who'd run, prisoners who hadn't tried to escape.

Rat-tat-tat-tat! The SS man shot them too. Then the solider turned the gun on us in the roll call ranks. *Rat-tat-tat-tat!* I closed my eyes and prayed the bullets wouldn't find me, trembling as prisoners were hit and fell dead to the ground all around me. I couldn't move though. I couldn't run. If I flinched, I would be singled out and shot.

"This is the punishment for escape! All of you will share the blame!" the watch officer yelled. He shot until the machine gun ran out of bullets. *Click-click-click.*

The SS officer threw his weapon to the ground. "Clean up this mess," he ordered, and he marched away, leaving us to carry away our own dead.

That night, in what little sleeping time there was left, I dreamed that Amon Goeth was chasing me with his dogs. I ran, and ran, and ran, but I could never quite get away. Then one of the dogs leaped and bit my left arm. I woke up screaming and holding my burning left arm — my left arm, where the Nazis had carved *B-3087* into my skin.

AUSCHWITZ
CONCENTRATION CAMP

1945

CHAPTER NINETEEN

AFTER A FEW MONTHS AT BIRKENAU, WE WERE told Auschwitz needed workers. Since Auschwitz was nearby, a sister camp to Birkenau, they marched us down the road and across the fields to get there. Our kapo stopped us at the station, where we waited for new prisoners to join us. You could tell they were new because they stepped off the trains in real clothes, not camp uniforms, with their luggage and children in tow.

"Leave your luggage!" the Nazis told them.

"Why? We were told to bring it with us," they argued.

The Nazis promised them it would all be returned to them in due time, and the new prisoners believed them. The Nazis loved having new prisoners who didn't know what was coming. It amused them. I could only feel sorry for these new arrivals. They had no idea the waking nightmare that lay in wait for them.

"Have you heard of Auschwitz?" our kapo asked the new prisoners. "No? Someone's waiting for you inside. Do you know who? Death, of course. Death waits for you. Look and see."

The new prisoners kept their distance from us veteran prisoners as we were herded toward the main gate. They looked at us with wide eyes, and pulled their children away from us. Did we look like monsters to them? I glanced around at the other prisoners who had come with me from Birkenau. We were skin and bones, with shaved heads and shuffling gaits and red skin on our arms where they'd tattooed us. Our eyes were sunk into our heads, our ears stuck out like donkey ears, and we must have smelled wretched, though of course we'd all been long accustomed to our stench. I was fifteen—maybe sixteen?—and I looked like a sixty-year-old man. To these people just off the train, we all must have looked like escaped mental-asylum patients with our shaved heads and our wooden shoes and oversized blue-and-gray-striped uniforms.

If only they knew that *this* was what awaited them. If they weren't taken right to the gas chambers and the furnaces.

We passed under the front gates of Auschwitz, where the German words ARBEIT MACHT FREI were written above the gate. I knew enough German to translate it: *Work makes you free.*

A smiling SS guard told us a very different story as we passed. "You come in through the front gate," he said, "but the only way out is through the chimney."

I looked up with the new prisoners to the tops of the brick chimneys, where a thick black smoke poured out into the blue-white sky. The crematorium. Little flecks of gray fluttered down all around us, collecting on puddles of water in the yard. I watched a little girl in a blue dress catch one on her tongue like snow. I didn't have the heart to tell her it was the ashes of the people who had come before us.

I recognized the assembly yard before they ever told us what it was. They all looked the same: a big muddy field surrounded by barbed-wire fence, with a bullet-ridden brick wall especially for executions. Auschwitz prisoners in charge of crowd control organized us into a single-file line. One of them shambled up the line, whispering urgent advice. "You're eighteen, you're in good health, and you have a trade. You're eighteen, you're in good health, and you have a trade."

"What?" said the man in front of me. He wore black trousers and a black vest over a clean white shirt, and he stood with his wife and their young son. The boy couldn't have been more than ten. "What did that man say? Why should I tell them I'm eighteen?"

"Your boy," I said. "Tell them your boy is eighteen and has a trade."

They recoiled when they saw me, monster that I was. *See if you don't look the same in a year*, I thought.

"What? But that's preposterous. He's nine. He's just a boy," the woman said.

I left it. A Nazi soldier was walking by, and I wasn't going to get caught talking.

We had been lined up so someone at the table ahead could process us, and slowly I made my way to the front. Three Nazi officers sat at the table. The two officers on the sides wore brown shirts and pants, but the man in the middle wore the black of a senior officer. He looked immaculate, with a shining black cap, polished medals, and neat white gloves like a traffic policeman. No one was so clean in a camp, ever, not even the camp commandants. This was a man of importance, I could tell right away. He held a baton in his right hand, and with a flick of it to the left or right he was separating the line.

One direction, I knew, would be for the camp work detail. The other would be for the furnaces.

"Good material this time," I heard him say as we got closer.

"Yes, Herr Doctor Mengele," one of the brown-shirts told him.

"Next," Mengele told the family in front of me. "How old are you?"

"I am thirty-nine, my wife is thirty-six, and our son is nine," the man told Mengele.

"Are you healthy?" Mengele asked the man.

"Y-yes. Only my wife had pneumonia recently, and she is still weak from it."

I closed my eyes. The man was telling them too much, and not the right things.

"Your occupation?" Mengele asked.

"I am a clerk."

"Not anymore," Mengele told him. He waved his baton to the right for the man, and to the left for the woman and the little boy. Kapos came and pulled them apart.

"Wait! Where are you taking them?" the man asked, looking terrified.

"Papa!" the boy cried. He reached for his father, but an SS officer pulled him and his mother away while another officer pushed the father to the right.

"Next," Mengele said to me. "How old are you?"

I stood as tall as I could. "Eighteen," I lied.

"Are you healthy?"

"As an ox," I lied again. It was all I could do not to waver as I stood.

"What is your occupation?"

I could hardly tell them "student." The man before had said "clerk," and he'd been lucky they'd kept him. "Bricklayer," I lied again.

Herr Doctor Mengele pointed his baton to the right, and I joined the ranks of the other men and women who'd been kept to work. At least I hoped that was the group I had been assigned to. Beside the new prisoners, the older prisoners like me looked pathetically weak and incapable of any kind of real labor.

"Where are they taking my wife and son?" the man who had been ahead of me asked a kapo.

The kapo cuffed him with his club, making the man's lip bleed. "They're going to the gas chambers! Now shut up unless you want to join them."

For a moment, it looked like the man might say that he would.

"Save your own life," someone whispered behind him. "Just let them go. It's better for them this way."

"How can I let them go?" the man cried. "They're my family. I love them."

But he stayed where he was, holding the back of his hand to his bleeding lip as he wept.

When the selection was finished, one of the brownshirts addressed our group. Herr Doctor Mengele was done for the day.

"Prisoners!" the brownshirt said. "You are fortunate. You are strong enough to have been selected for work. Once all the Jews of Europe are collected into our camps, we will organize a new Jewish state for you, where you will be free."

The new prisoners looked at one another hopefully. Some of them, like the man who'd been in front of me in line, no doubt thought this meant that his wife and son were still alive, and just taken to a different part of the camp. They didn't know the games the Nazis played yet. The lies they told us for sport.

"You will be happy to know too that your stay here in the camp will cost you nothing. All the valuables you brought with you are at this moment being distributed among the camps, where they will be used exclusively for the benefit of the Jews."

Another lie. At Birkenau, we had seen the stockpiles of riches in "Canada," the camp storehouse. We had seen how the Nazis made the warehouse their own personal shopping center before shipping trainloads of gold and silver back to Berlin.

"Work," the officer urged us. "Work will set you free. If you work hard, if you perform your duties faithfully, you may be attached to the Wehrmacht as service personnel. From there, you may even earn positions of authority within the new Jewish state."

The new prisoners nodded, buying it hook, line, and sinker. I didn't have the heart to tell any of the new Jews it was all a pack of lies when the roll call was finished and we were sent to our new barracks. No one did. The new prisoners would learn soon enough, and they would accept the truth or they would die.

That night as I lay in the middle slot of my three-tiered bunk, I heard voices in the distance singing. I couldn't believe it, and I lifted my head to hear better. It was a lullaby my mother had sung to me when I was a child, but it sounded like it was being sung by a choir. Had I finally lost my mind? Was I going crazy?

"It's the women," the man next to me in the bunk whispered. "They sing when mothers and their children are taken to the gas chambers."

I listened to their song, distant and plaintive.

"How often do they sing?" I asked.

"All day," the man said. "All day, and every night."

CHAPTER TWENTY

SOMETIMES IN THE MORNING, PRISONERS DIDN'T wake up.

They were dead. Or dying. The guards would come in and beat their bodies to make sure they weren't faking it, and while we were gone to roll call or on a work detail the bodies would disappear, carted off to the furnaces to burn like the rest.

One morning the man in the bunk next to me didn't wake. I knew what death looked like by now. Death and I had become old acquaintances. We knew each other when we passed on the street. This man was dead, I was sure.

"What is it?" another prisoner asked me. He was a boy, like me, maybe one or two years older.

"This man is dead," I told him.

The boy poked him to be sure, then looked around to see if the kapos were coming yet.

"Go through his pockets," he said

"What?" I was momentarily surprised by his words.

"See if he still has any bread on him."

It sounded awful, but if the man did have food on him he definitely didn't need it anymore. I put my hands in the pockets of his striped jacket and found a lice-ridden piece of bread from last night's dinner. I brushed off the lice, tore the bread in half, and gave half to the other boy. We scarfed down the bread before the kapos came.

The boy introduced himself to me as Fred. I told him my name—Yanek. Not B-3087. I hadn't spoken my name to anyone for as long as I could remember. Fred and I shook hands. It was the first intentional contact I'd had with anyone at the camps since Uncle Moshe had died. We were all the time touching other people—lined up at roll call, at work, in line to get food, in bed at night. But I hadn't shaken hands or hugged anyone on purpose in months. It felt good to connect with someone, even though Uncle Moshe's words came back to me again: *You have no name, no*

personality, no family, no friends. Nothing to iden-
tify you, nothing to care about. Not if you want to
survive.

Fred and I stood together at roll call, but of course we didn't say a word to each other the whole time. When it was time for work detail, we were assigned together to the gravel pit, where we worked side by side breaking rocks.

"Where are you from?" Fred asked me while we worked.

I hesitated, remembering Uncle Moshe's warnings. But Fred was the first person close to my age I'd met since hiding under the floors at Plaszów with Isaac and Thomas. I loved just talking again. Being human.

"Kraków," I told him.

"Me too!" Fred said. We compared streets, and discovered we had grown up not too far from each other. We even went to some of the same parks and stores. "Every day I would walk my sister to school down Krakusa Street," he said, remembering. Then he got very quiet.

"Where is she now?" I asked.

"She and my parents came here with me. I was sent to the right. They were sent to the left."

I knew what that meant. We all did. His family was dead.

Overhead, we heard the drone of airplanes, and we all looked up.

"British planes," someone whispered. I didn't know how they could tell, but I hoped they were right. British planes meant the Allies were advancing, taking the fight to the Germans. The Allies were the forces aligned against Germany—England, France, America, and the rest.

The kapos cracked their whips and made us all get back to work, but soon we heard explosions in the distance. The Allies were bombing close by!

"Sometimes I wish the Allies would drop bombs on us," Fred said quietly. "Blow this place to bits, and all the Nazis and kapos with it. And me too."

"We can't give up," I told him. "We have to survive."

Fred tried to smile, but I could tell he was still thinking about his family. He didn't say anything more the rest of the morning. It was only at lunch that he felt like talking again. He lifted a spoonful of the tepid, flavorless broth and poured it back into his bowl.

"You know what I'm going to do first thing, when I get out of the camps? I'm going to buy a big, warm, golden loaf of bread. Then I'm going to slice off a thick piece, and I'm going to spread butter all over it and eat it in three bites."

I laughed. "I'll take five pastries. Oh, and bagels. Three of those."

"With cream cheese!"

"Carrot cake with walnuts."

"Chocolate pudding!"

Just talking about all that delicious food made my stomach rumble, but it was fun to dream. We kept up our running menu all through work in the gravel pit that afternoon, and into the evening in the barracks while we lay next to each other on our shelf.

"Fresh challah bread!" I said.

"Sauerkraut."

"Mushroom soup."

"Stuffed cabbage."

"Will you two shut up about food?" a prisoner near us yelled at last. "I can't stand it any longer!"

Fred and I laughed, but we stopped. It was best that we got as much sleep as we could anyway. We had a hard day's work ahead of us, and nothing good to eat.

Fred and I became inseparable in the camp. We stood together at roll call, we ate together, we tried to get on the same work details, we slept beside each other at night. It was good to have a friend. But one day I noticed Fred was slower at chopping wood than he had been the day before, and at dinner he wouldn't eat his bread.

"What's wrong, Fred?"

"I don't feel good," he told me. He gave me his bread and climbed up into bed. I saved the bread for him in my pocket. He would want it tomorrow, I was sure.

But he didn't want it then. He didn't eat his soup at lunch either. I had to do some of his work at the timber yard to cover for him too. That night as we lay on our shelf, I whispered to him that he had to get better.

"I can't, Yanek. It hurts."

"What does?"

"My stomach. My head. My throat."

Fred was sick, there was no doubt about it. But you couldn't get sick in the camps. Not so sick you couldn't work. There was a camp clinic, but no one wanted to go there. People didn't come back from the camp clinic.

"You'll be better tomorrow," I told Fred. "I saved you some bread for when you're better."

Fred wasn't better the next day. He was worse. He couldn't even get out of bed.

"Fred, you have to get up!" I told him. "You have to move! The kapo will come for you soon!"

"No," Fred moaned. "No, Yanek. Go. You have to. Go."

"What's this? What's going on?" an angry voice demanded. It was our barrack kapo. He pushed me aside and poked Fred with his club. "Get up. Time for roll call."

"He can't," I told the kapo. "He's sick."

The kapo struck me with his club, sending me to the floor. I put my hand to my ear and felt blood.

"Get up!" the kapo told Fred again. He hit him with the club, and Fred moaned.

I stood up and was about to grab the kapo to try and stop him, but another prisoner took me by the arm. "Come away," he whispered. "Come away, boy."

The kapo hit Fred again, and again.

"Fred!" I yelled.

"Get to roll call, or you'll get a beating!" the kapo threatened me.

"Yanek," Fred moaned. "Go. Please."

The kapo hit him again as the other prisoner pulled me away.

"He's going to kill him!" I pleaded with the man.

"Yes, and he'll kill you too if you interfere. Is that what you want?"

I stood in line at the roll call, watching for Fred. He had to get up. He could make it. He wasn't a Muselmann yet. He was just sick! He would get better!

Fred arrived at roll call at the very end, but only because he was dragged there by two kapos. His face was bloody where they'd beaten him, and he hung limp, not even trying to stand. I fought back the tears that came to my eyes.

The kapos hauled Fred to the front of the assembly yard, where a gallows was built. It was a simple thing: just two standing poles with a bar between them. From the pole hung a rope with a noose tied at the end. The two kapos lifted Fred's neck into the noose and tightened it, leaving a chair under his feet to keep him from hanging. He was so weak he couldn't even stand, and the rope cut into his neck, turning his face blue. I choked back a sob.

"This man says he cannot work," a Nazi told us.

No, I thought. *No, he can. He's a good worker. He's just sick.*

"Work makes you free," the Nazi told us. "But if you cannot work—"

The Nazi nodded to the kapos, and one of them kicked the chair out from under Fred. He lifted his head for just a moment, long enough for me to see his horrified face, and then I couldn't watch anymore.

That night I said a kaddish for Fred as I ate his bread, and made another vow never to forget.

DEATH MARCH

1945

CHAPTER TWENTY-ONE

ONE MORNING AFTER ROLL CALL AT AUSCHWITZ, we were told we were being moved. All of us. I had never counted, but there had to be five thousand of us at roll call every day, give or take a few hundred. Workers were needed in the Sachsenhausen concentration camp, the officer of the watch told us, and we were being sent to fill their barracks.

I could feel the other prisoners tensing around me. If we could have whispered and talked, we would have. Every day, Allied planes flew overhead, and the bombs they dropped got closer. Sometimes at night we would even hear the sound of guns. Big guns. Tank guns, antiaircraft guns. At the beginning of the war, the Germans had taken the fight to France, to Belgium, to Holland, to Russia. Now the fight was happening in Germany. So when the Nazis said they were moving us to Sachsenhausen because the camp needed workers, none of us believed them. The Allies were getting closer. They were pushing back! Any day now we might be liberated. That was the talk in the barracks. The Nazis were probably moving us away from the front lines.

There were no trains to take us to Sachsenhausen, the watch officer told us, so we would walk. That was another good sign for the end of the war, if the Germans had to use all their trains for the war effort. But it was bad for us. I had no idea where Sachsenhausen was, or how far we would have to go, but just the thought of walking all day made me feel exhausted. There were others, I knew, who would never make it a kilometer. But walk we would, some in bare feet and some in odd-sized wooden clogs, in our thin uniforms, in the middle of winter.

The Nazis gave us each a half a loaf of bread, and told us it was to last us the whole trip. But how many days would that be? None of us dared ask. I decided right away that I would eat just a bit of my bread at a time, to make it last. If I ended up with extra, I would eat the rest at Sachsenhausen.

Under the whips and clubs of kapos and SS officers, we marched out through the front of Auschwitz.

You come in through the front gate, but the only way you leave is through the chimney, the guards had told us when we arrived. *Ha! Look at me now,* I wanted to shout, *walking out through the front gate, the way I came in!* I had survived the ghetto. I had survived Plaszów, and Wieliczka, and Trzebinia, and Birkenau, and now Auschwitz. I was going to survive it all. I was going to be alive when the Allies liberated us. This I swore.

But nothing had prepared me for the death march. That is what we began to call it, as our numbers dwindled. We marched for hours upon hours each day, stumbling and staggering along as best we could. We walked, and we walked, and we walked, and I began to think there was no Sachsenhausen. That the Nazis merely meant to walk us to death. Those who could not keep up were shot and left by the roadside. The crack of guns behind us was our constant companion, and you knew you had slowed too much if the guns got too loud.

Snow fell on us most days, and the dirt road we walked on was frozen when we were lucky, freezing slush when we were not. Those without shoes were the first to fall behind and die. Some tore strips from their canvas jackets and wrapped them around their bare feet, but once the canvas got wet it was worse. I at least had wooden clogs to keep my feet off the frozen earth, but without socks my feet were blocks of ice anyway.

There was no water. We ate snow when we stopped for the night, caught flakes on our tongues as we walked. We slept in the open when there was no barn or shed to be found, which was most nights, sleeping on top of one another like dogs for the warmth. The kapos and Nazis had fires to keep them warm. At least in the camps we had shelter to keep the weather off us at night. Out here, the elements killed more prisoners than our guards did.

On the fifth day—or was it the sixth? I had lost count—I woke up and I was sure I couldn't go on any farther. My arms and legs were so cold I couldn't make them move in the morning, and I was sure a Nazi would shoot me. But there were others like me, many others. One man's ear had frozen to the ground in the night. The Nazis gave us time to wake and stir before resuming the march, which was a small mercy. Perhaps they just didn't have bullets for us all.

As we shambled along later that day, I looked at the men around me. We were skeletons. Ghosts. Filthy toothless creatures in oversized, soiled prisoner uniforms. The hair on our heads was growing in thin and scraggly from not-too-recent shavings. Our fingers were long and bony like vampires from some Hollywood horror movie, the skin on our faces cracked and drawn back like mummies. The older men had the beginnings of beards on their gray skin, and we all walked like zombies, stumbling more than striding, trying always to stay just one step ahead of the Nazis and their guns.

Not long ago, all these half-dead creatures around me had been people, I realized. Which of them had been doctors? Teachers? Musicians? Businessmen, like my father? Which of the boys had been students like me? Playing ball in the streets after school, laughing and calling to their friends?

It seemed like a lifetime ago. Years. How many years? Like the days, I was beginning to lose count. Five years? Six? Had it been that long? I had been ten when the war started. That made me sixteen years old now. I should almost be done with school and thinking about a career, or maybe even university. Mother and Father had always wanted me to go to university. But there had been plenty of time to think about that, once. Years and years to prepare. Years that were gone now. Stolen from me by the Nazis.

I closed my eyes, half-walking and half-sleeping, listening always for the crack of the guns at my heels to know when to pick up my pace. There was the danger of passing out, of being shot while I slept, but I couldn't help it. I had only half my bread left, tucked into the waist of my pants. I had stretched it as far as it would go, and still I had no energy left to walk.

Something droned in the distance, and our shambling column—so much smaller now than when we had begun our journey—slowed to look up. Three enormous planes flew by, high up in the clouds, raining tiny black specks from their bellies.

Bombs. They were Allied planes, dropping bombs somewhere in the distance! We heard the rumble of explosions and saw smoke rise over a hill on the horizon. I wanted to cheer them on, to raise my fists and cry, *"Yes! Yes! Stick it to the Nazis!"* but I knew I had to keep silent. I wasn't sure I had the strength to shout anyway. The kapos cracked their whips and we got moving again, but secretly I was still urging the Allies on to victory.

One of the prisoners began to sing. He was Czech, I think. It sounded like Czech, from what I'd heard of it in the camps. *"Bejvavalo dobre, bejvavalo dobre,"* he sang, his voice weak but insistent. *"Za nasich mladejch let, bejval svet jako kvet."* I tensed, sure one of the soldiers would shoot him, but they let him continue. Another prisoner, another Czech farther along the line, joined him, and then another behind me. Then a Pole beside me began to sing, and I recognized the refrain: *"Hey, hey, hey falcons, pass the mountains, forests, pits. Ring, ring, ring my little bell, in the steppe, ring, ring, ring. Sorry, sorry for the girl, for the green Ukraine. Sorry, sorry your heart is weeping. I'll never see you again."*

Another Pole took up "Hey, falcons!" with him, and then there was a chorus. Then the German Jews began to sing a different song, and the Italian Jews another. I heard a Dutch voice, and an English one, and behind me came the most beautiful French voice I had ever heard, though I didn't understand a word of his song. We sang as we walked, all of us, singing a hundred different songs, and the Nazis let us sing. Another small mercy. Or perhaps they too missed the way the world had been before the war.

CHAPTER TWENTY-TWO

NINE DAYS INTO OUR LONG MARCH—OR WAS IT ten?—I found myself walking next to another boy about my age. His face was red and his eyes were half shut, and he staggered with each step. He was about as close to a Muselmann as you can get without actually being one, without crumpling to the ground and not being able to get up again. He almost swayed into me once, so I picked up my pace and got ahead of him.

I couldn't stop thinking about him though. He reminded me of Fred, sick in his bed and not able to get up and work. Fred, who had been such a friend to me when I had so desperately wanted one, *needed* one, at Auschwitz. I kept looking back at the boy, watching him weave through the shuffling lines. Once, he stumbled and fell, only climbing back to his feet after a struggle. Very soon now he would be at the back of the lines, where the SS and their pistols waited.

I couldn't help it. I had to go back to him. I slowed down until we were alongside each other.

"Hey," I said. "Hey—you have to walk faster."

The boy said nothing. There was no life in his eyes, no hint that he'd even heard me. I grabbed his arm.

"Hey, listen to me. Just one more day, yes? You can make it one more day, and then you can sleep tonight, and start tomorrow fresh. You just have to keep walking."

The boy tripped and stumbled into me, and I caught him. I propped him up under his shoulder, letting him lean on me, but he never broke away. Perhaps his body knew that if he let go, he would fall again. He slumped against me, and suddenly I was carrying half the boy's weight. He wasn't really heavy—none of us were anymore—but I was already so weak and tired from the march and from eating my bread sparingly that I barely had the strength to carry myself. Within just a few meters I stumbled under the weight of him, but I didn't let go.

What was I doing? Had I gone crazy? Uncle Moshe would be scolding me right now. I could hear his voice. *We have only one purpose now:* survive. *Survive at all costs, Yanek.* Each step I took was harder than the last. Why was I wasting my energy carrying along a sick boy who would most likely be dead before we got to Sachsenhausen? I hadn't thought this through, and now here I was holding the boy up.

I should let him go, I thought over and over. *Let him make his own way. I should save myself.* That was how you survived the camps: You saved yourself. No one else was going to do it for you.

But this boy had a face. He had a name too, though I didn't know it. He had a mother and father, probably dead now, but he had family. A home somewhere. He could have been me. He could have been Yanek Gruener, son of Oskar and Mina, of 20 Krakusa Street, Podgórze, Kraków. If it were me, wouldn't I want someone to help me? Even if I was out of my mind with hunger and exhaustion, wouldn't I want the boy who was helping me to stay there under my arm, to help me just a little farther along the way?

Surely somebody else had to feel the same way. If I could just find someone to help me, if we shared the load, we would all make it, even this nameless boy.

"Please," I said to the man nearest me. "Please help me."

The man heard me, but he wouldn't look at me. Instead he picked up his pace and left us behind.

"Just help me carry him," I begged another man.

"Don't be a fool," the man said, and he too moved away.

"Leave him," another prisoner told me.

"He's going to die anyway," said another. "Let him go, or he'll take you with him."

Crack! I jumped. Somewhere behind us another prisoner had fallen too far behind, and the Nazis had shot him. They would shoot me too if we fell behind, even though I wasn't the sick one.

Why wouldn't someone help us? It didn't have to be this way, every man for himself! If we all helped one another, if we became one another's family now, when all of our real families had been taken from us, we could be stronger! More of us could survive! But too many of them thought like Uncle Moshe. Too many of them would only look out for themselves. I wanted to yell at them, argue with them, but I was too tired. It wouldn't do any good anyway. I was right, but so were they, in their way. The only person you could trust in the camps was yourself.

I should never have helped the boy. I knew that. But now that I was helping him, I refused to let him go. I was becoming stubborn now that I was sixteen. I walked along, giving the nameless boy all the energy I could spare. I longed to have a bite of my bread, but it was tucked into the waistband of my pants behind my back, and I couldn't reach it and carry the boy at the same time. I would have to wait for nightfall and our scheduled stop before I could eat again. It was better that way, I figured. My bread would last longer. So long as I survived to eat it.

But as we walked along, step after step, kilometer after kilometer, my stomach began to gnaw away at itself. I was so hungry! Just a bite of bread, just a pinch, and I could quiet my aching stomach for a few more hours. The only way to eat was to let go of the boy though, and we were already near the back of the lines. I couldn't stop. But I was so hungry I cried.

The gray clouds in the sky meant more snow, but they also meant night would come earlier, and maybe an earlier end to the day's marching. *Just a little farther*, I told myself. *One more step. Then another.* If I fell, it would be hard for me to get up again—and impossible for me to lift the boy. If I dropped him now, all this torture would have been for nothing, and that seemed worse than having helped him to begin with.

But I wasn't going to make it to nightfall, not even with the gray clouds overhead. Just when I thought I couldn't take another step, my load lightened — another prisoner stepped in to take the boy's other arm! He was an old man with sunken, bloodshot eyes, deep cracks in his face, and a grizzled beard. He looked like I might be carrying him next.

"Can't walk so well myself," he rasped, "but I'll help you the rest of the way today."

Tears streamed down my face. I should have said thank you, but I was too tired to speak. The old man seemed to understand. "Keep walking," he told me. We walked along in silence the rest of the evening, the only sounds the crunch of the frozen mud beneath our feet and the cracks of the kapos' whips. I tried to block out everything else and focused on putting one foot in front of the other. It was still a struggle to carry the boy, but with someone else to help I was rejuvenated.

Darkness had long since fallen when we reached the top of a hill and found no barn or house in sight. The guards stopped us and told us the frozen ground would once again be our bed. None of us complained. My companion and I dropped the boy to the ground as quickly as we could, and before I could thank him he disappeared into the crowd of prisoners huddling together for warmth as they slept. I stood over the boy a moment longer, wondering what his name was, and if he would even survive the night. His breath was ragged, and his body barely moved. Had I used up all that energy for nothing?

Before I could sleep, I had to eat. I reached for what was left of my half loaf of bread tucked into my pants, but it wasn't there! In a panic, I patted all around my waistline, even checking to see if it had slid down inside my pants. I was so cold and my pants were so big I might not have noticed. But there was nothing there. My bread was gone! It must have slid out while I was carrying the boy, and I hadn't noticed. Half of my food, lost! And who knew how much longer we would be walking? I fell to my knees, sobbing. Without food, I would never survive.

I looked down at the nameless boy again, and my hands made fists. I wanted to hit him. It was all his fault! I would never have wasted all that energy, would never have lost my food, if it wasn't for him! But I pounded my own bony legs instead. It wasn't the boy's fault. It was mine, and I knew it.

And then I saw it. A lump in the boy's pocket. What was left of his bread. It was as much as I'd lost, maybe more. I reached a hand out to take the bread from the boy's pocket, but I stopped. Had it come to this? Was I so desperate to survive that I would steal bread from a sick boy? I quickly moved behind the boy and nestled in close, so we could keep each other warm in the night. But as I lay there under the starless black sky, my stomach moaning—or was it me moaning?—all I could think about was that bit of bread. So little I might have left it on my plate after dinner once, a long time ago, before the war. But now that little bit of bread was everything. It was the difference between life and death.

He's sick, I told myself. *He's mostly dead already. He's a Muselmann. In the morning he won't be able to get up, and they'll shoot him where he lies. He doesn't need that bread. It would probably make him sick to eat it now anyway. If I take it, at least one of us will survive.*

Face it, I told myself. *He'll be dead by morning.*

Still, I couldn't take it. Not when I could feel him breathing, not when I could feel his heart beating in his bony chest. He might die by morning. Probably would. But I could wait until then. I would not steal bread from another living prisoner. Instead I closed my eyes and hoped that sleep would at least let me forget my hunger for a few hours.

———

It was my stomach that woke me the next morning, more than the light. My first thought was the boy's bread, but the rise and fall of the boy's chest told me he hadn't died in the night. He was still alive! How was it possible? And not only was he alive, but his breath was much less shallow. There was color in his face again too. The sleep had done what I promised him it would — it had given him the rest he needed to face a new day of marching.

I shook with anger and frustration. He was supposed to die! I needed him to die, so I could have his bread.

I closed my eyes. What was I thinking? I wouldn't steal bread from a living boy, but I would wish death on him so I could take it without guilt? What were the camps doing to me? What had the Nazis turned me into?

Faced with two evils — stealing from a living boy, or wishing him dead to take his food guilt-free — I realized I could more easily have the sin of stealing on my conscience. I needed that bread to live, and I was going to take it. The boy *owed* me, after all. He was alive only because I had helped him.

Slowly, my hand shaking, I reached around the nameless boy for the bread sticking out of his pocket. I touched it. I had it in my fingers when the boy's eyes opened wide and he stirred.

"Hey! What are you doing?" he said.

I yanked my hand back. "Nothing! I was—I was just trying to see if you were still alive."

The boy pushed the bread farther down into his pocket. "Well, I am," the boy told me. He pushed himself to his feet.

"Wait," I said. "I'm the one who helped you yesterday—" I started to say, but without so much as a thank-you the boy staggered away to join the march.

I would have cried again, but I was too tired. A kapo came around, kicking the last of us still on the ground, and I picked myself up. I wasn't a Muselmann. I might be starving, and I might be that nameless boy the others saw staggering through the ranks by midday, but I wasn't dead yet. My name was still Yanek, and I was going to survive.

SACHSENHAUSEN
CONCENTRATION CAMP

1945

CHAPTER TWENTY-THREE

THREE DAYS LATER, I STAGGERED THROUGH THE gates of Sachsenhausen. I barely knew where I was, or who I was. All I remembered of the last three days was an enormous radio tower in the distance, growing larger and larger as we marched. "That's Berlin," someone had said. "That tower is in Berlin." The tower was in Berlin, but we weren't; we were in Sachsenhausen, and I was so tired and hungry that I didn't care if I lived or died. Death seemed like such a welcome release.

If the Nazis had put us right to work, I might have died that day. I might have curled up on the ground like a Muselmann and never gotten up again. But they sent us to our barracks instead, where they fed us soup and bread. I was starving—I had been without food for days now, with only snow to eat each morning before we began to walk again—but all I wanted to do was sleep. When would they let us lie down?

They wouldn't let us get into our bunks yet, so I sipped at the soup. It was nothing better than flavored water, but it was warm. So blessedly warm! My dry mouth tried to hang on to every last drop as I swallowed it down. The bread I couldn't eat. Not yet. I didn't put it in the waist of my pants this time though. I clung to it like it was a precious jewel, hoarding it like a dragon.

At last they told us it was time to sleep, and I crawled up into a single bed with five other men. There were so many of us we couldn't sleep on our backs, but I fell asleep right away just the same. Just being out of the cold felt like paradise.

It seemed I had just closed my eyes when morning came and the kapos roused us up out of our beds. In the light of day, we could see the camp was filled with corpses. Sometimes they lay alone, up against the wall of a barrack, as though they had simply fallen asleep there. Sometimes there were piles of them, built neatly in rows of four, one level turned this way, the next level turned that way, so they would stack evenly. Sometimes the bodies looked like they had just been tossed aside where they had died, in the middle of a path, out behind the latrine. I had seen death many times by now. I had seen men killed, and I had watched men die of starvation and cold right in front of me. But here in Sachsenhausen, death was so common, so ordinary, that the dead were like fallen trees in the forest — so unremarkable that they were only moved when they got in the way.

Before roll call we would wash, the Nazis told us, and they marched us out to some pumps. There were no brushes, no soap, no towels, but I rinsed myself off anyway. The water was freezing, but I was filthy from the march. As I ran a wet finger across my teeth, a memory suddenly came to me, unbidden. I remembered the first day my mother had brought me home a toothbrush. I must have been no more than three or four. The toothbrush was shiny and plastic and green. That moment seemed like a million years ago. Had I ever really owned something so amazing as a toothbrush? Had I ever really lived in a world with such wondrous things in it? Even the simplest of possessions seemed like treasures now.

On the way to roll call, I ate what I could of last night's bread. I had clutched it throughout the night, and woke to find myself still protecting it. The soup and sleep and bread had done me good. I was no prize now, all bones and skin and shaking hands, but I wasn't so far gone that I couldn't work.

The Nazis lined us up for roll call near the front gate, which had the words *Work Makes You Free* on it, just like at Auschwitz. Our new masters didn't seem interested in making us work though. Not right away. Instead we stood at attention, our feet sinking into the freezing mud while they called our numbers. Again and again they went through the roll call.

Sleet began to fall, and the Nazis left us standing in the yard while they went inside to warm themselves by the fire. They watched us from the windows, making sure none of us moved. We stood there for hours, for no reason other than the delight of our captors.

One man wiped the wet sleet from his face, and the Nazis saw him. They rushed outside and beat him, then ordered him to give what they called the Sachsenhausen salute. They forced him to squat with his hands held out in front of him. If he moved in any way, if his arms lowered, or his legs moved, or he fell over on his side, the Nazis would kill him. And they never let him up, either. It was torture. Everyone could see that. Our legs were barely strong enough to hold us up, let alone to squat for hours. Even a healthy person would fall over in time. The man's legs began to shake, and his arms started to quiver, but still he held the salute. It was only later, when the Nazis had resumed the roll call and we had all forgotten about him, that the man finally fell over. The Nazis ran to beat him, but he never felt it. He was unconscious. Maybe even dead. I didn't know. The guards dragged him away, and I never saw him again.

Suddenly one of the prisoners near the end of the line broke off and ran. The Nazis saw him right away and yelled for the guards at the gate to catch him, but he wasn't headed for the gate. In a stumbling, broken run, the prisoner threw himself on the high-voltage electric barbed wire that lined the fence. His body sparked and thrashed in the wires and bled as the barbs cut him. Within seconds his body hung dead and limp. The Nazis had to turn off the electric fence to get him out. His shirt and pants were scorched from the electricity, and his skin was black where the wires had touched him. I couldn't look, but at the same time I couldn't look away.

The Germans laughed as they threw his body down in front of us for everyone to see.

"Would any other Jews like to throw themselves on the fence?" they asked. "Go now! We won't stop you! We'll be glad to be rid of you!"

No one else took them up on their offer.

After roll call we were finally put to work. I broke rocks again in the quarry pit. Why the Germans needed so much gravel I never understood, but I broke big rocks into medium-sized rocks, and medium-sized rocks into small rocks, and small rocks into gravel for them—*pound, pound, pound, pound*—my hammer getting heavier and heavier with each strike.

At lunch, a half dozen other young men and I were pulled away from our scant meals of watery soup and hard bread. We looked at one another nervously. Was this it? Were we all going to be lined up along a trench and shot? I fought down waves of terror as I walked. Had I survived the death march and gotten my strength back, such as it was, all so I could die in a muddy ditch? I didn't want to die. Not after surviving so long. Not after coming so far. I scanned the camp as we walked, watching for where they were taking us. If it was a death pit, what would I do? Run? Turn and fight? Yell and scream? Or would I let them shoot me without fighting back, so that no one else would have to suffer because of me?

But it wasn't a ditch the Nazis took us to. It was the soldiers' mess hall. I was even more confused. Were they going to feed us? In the soldiers' canteen?

No. It was a trick, of course. All part of the Nazis' game. And in Sachsenhausen, they played the game with relish. The other boys and I were lined up in front of the soldiers' tables, and we were told to sing. For an hour we were their choir, our weak, raspy voices serenading them as they laughed and talked and ate — and the food they ate! Big, heaping plates of meat and potatoes and gravy, and steaming black coffee. I tried to look away so my stomach wouldn't rumble, but just the smell of it made my mouth water. They weren't going to feed us any of it, of course. When they were finished eating we were sent back to our barracks, where we found no food left for us.

That afternoon, they put me to work chopping firewood to heat the soldiers' quarters. *Chop, chop, chop, chop.* Every swing meant survival, I told myself. *Work to live. Live until the Allies come.* There were planes overhead here too, and the rumbles of explosions in the distance. Berlin was under attack. The war had come to Germany. But would the war end before the Nazis killed me?

That night at roll call the Sachsenhausen guards wanted entertainment, so they had a boxing tournament. They made some of the prisoners be the boxers and forced the rest of us to watch.

BERGEN-BELSEN CONCENTRATION CAMP

1945

CHAPTER TWENTY-FOUR

WHEN THE GUARDS AT SACHSENHAUSEN TIRED of us, they shipped us off by train to Bergen-Belsen. We traveled by cattle car again, and again prisoners died of starvation and suffocation along the way. Once the Nazis dropped three loaves of bread in our car through a hole at the top, just to watch us fight for it. As our train pushed farther north, there was more room to breathe as the dead dropped to the floor.

The train arrived at Bergen-Belsen in the morning, my seventh concentration camp in less than three years. The commandant of the camp took one look at us and started screaming at our guards. "What did you bring me? Look at these skeletons! How do you expect these walking dead to work?" The commandant moved among us, pointing at prisoners. "Him. Him. Him. Him," he said, and soldiers pulled the men out of the ranks. I puffed up my chest to try and look as strong and healthy as I could, but the commandant took one look at me and moved on past, picking other prisoners.

My heart cried out. No! I had to be strong enough to work! Work was the only way to survive!

When the commandant had pulled seventy-five prisoners out of our lines, he had them marched to the other side of the tracks and ordered his soldiers to shoot them. They were gunned down before we surviving, wide-eyed prisoners even had time to react. I quickly turned away. I couldn't watch. The commandant hadn't chosen the strongest, he'd taken the weakest. I just couldn't tell the difference. How he could, I didn't understand. I felt terrible for it, but secretly I was glad it had been somebody else who was killed, and not me.

"Take the others back to the barracks," the commandant said with disgust. "No work for a week, until they regain their strength."

I couldn't believe my ears. No work for a week? What kind of trick was this? I could see the other prisoners glancing at one another, wondering the same thing. But it was no trick. When we got back to the barracks, we were fed the thickest, richest soup I had eaten in six years, and big pieces of fresh bread, hot from the oven! I was so thin and miserable I thought I could gain weight just from the smell alone. There was no gas chamber here either, and no chimneys burning red in the night. Maybe Bergen-Belsen really was better than all the other camps. Maybe this was the place where I could survive until the war ended.

I scarfed my piece of bread and washed it down with that delicious, meaty soup, but an hour later I learned that even in kindness, the Nazis were cruel. Every one of us woke with the most terrible stomach cramps we'd ever had. Our poor stomachs weren't used to such hearty food. We spent the night changing places with one another on the two barrels left in the barrack. I finally drifted off close to dawn, still hunched over from the pain in my gut.

The next day they brought us more of the thick soup and warm bread, but this time I was careful. I remembered reading about medicine back in Kraków and learning that dry toast helped settle an upset stomach. So I traded my soup for more bread and toasted the bread over the wood stove in the barrack. I hated to give up the delicious soup, but the bread sat better with me, and I slowly began to get stronger.

A week later, as promised, we were put back to work. It was the same as always—chopping wood, breaking rocks, building new camp buildings. One day I was hard at work hauling boards for the walls of a barrack when one of our new kapos called me over. I studied him as I approached. He had a big, round face that was covered with acne pits and scars.

Without a word, he punched me in the face. My world exploded. Pain shot from my nose to my brain, and my head snapped back like I'd been hit with a shovel. I fell to the ground clutching my face.

"What did you do that for?" I cried. "What did I do?" I knew I shouldn't have said anything, but I didn't care. I was too stunned. My nose was already swelling up so badly I couldn't breathe through it.

"You looked at me the wrong way," the kapo told me. His eyes glittered with amusement before he told me to get up and get back to work.

My head was throbbing. It was hard to stand. Dark red blood splotched my blue-and-gray-striped uniform. I held the back of my sleeve to my nose—gently, tenderly, it still hurt so badly — trying to stem the bleeding. I hoped my nose wasn't broken. If it was, there was nothing I could do about it. I made it back to the boards I'd dropped, trying not to let my tears spill over.

"Moonface," one of the other prisoners said as he fell in alongside me.

"What?" I said.

"Moonface. That's what we call him." He nodded to the big, round-faced kapo who'd slugged me. "They say he killed three men before the war. The Germans put him in prison, but when the war started they made him a kapo. We've got murderers for guards."

I knew our guards were murderers now, but I didn't know some of them were convicted killers in the past. I made sure to stay well clear of Moonface after that, but somehow I always managed to be assigned to work duty near him. He seemed to notice me wherever I went too, and soon I became his pet project. Moonface kicked me and hit me and beat me whenever he could.

Bergen-Belsen might have been the place for me to survive until the end of the war, but for Moonface. I had to get away from him. When I heard the Nazis were rounding up workers to send them to another camp, I made sure I was at the front of the line. But the Nazis weren't looking for volunteers. They had their own method for choosing us already figured out.

"Only the strongest and healthiest prisoners will be transferred," the Nazi announced. "To prove which of you is most able, there will be a race."

More games. Each of us had to take off our clothes, roll them into bundles, and dash from one side of the barracks to the other. The Nazis watched and laughed as we staggered through the maze of beds. When it was my turn, I took off my uniform and was surprised, again, at how skinny I was. Even after a week of rest and better food, my arms and legs still looked like toothpicks.

"You!" one of the Nazis yelled at me. "Run!"

I ran as fast as I could. I had to win this race. I had to get out of Bergen-Belsen. I had to get away from Moonface! I was running for my life. I stumbled around one of the beds, and crashed into another, bruising my thigh very badly, but I still flew through the doorway at the other side of the barrack faster than some of the other prisoners. When I burst outside, all I wanted to do was collapse on the ground until my lungs stopped burning and my legs stopped shaking, but I knew if I did that the Nazis would never pick me to move on. Instead I forced myself to stand up and look relaxed, like I'd just taken a stroll in the park.

"He can work," one of the guards said.

I took my time putting my uniform back over my bony body, bending over so they couldn't see me gasping for breath. I spotted Moonface, out in the yard, pushing another prisoner to the ground and kicking him.

Another cattle car awaited me, and so did another camp, but at least I had gotten away from Moonface for good.

BUCHENWALD
CONCENTRATION CAMP

1945

CHAPTER TWENTY-FIVE

BUCHENWALD CONCENTRATION CAMP. JUST the looks on the faces of the prisoners already there told me all I needed to know. They were scared. Wide-eyed. And not just at roll call, or when a kapo passed by. It was all the time, like at any moment death might come for you. And at Buchenwald, as I was to learn, death came in many guises.

After our first roll call, I was assigned to the stone quarry. Instead of breaking rocks, I was told to carry them up a long hill. I had to carry the big rocks on my back, with my arms behind me to hold them in place. If you took a stone too large, you would drop it and the Nazis would shoot you. If you took a stone too small, the Nazis would shoot you for being lazy.

Picking just the right size stone became a kind of competition among us. Another fine joke from the Nazis.

Some of the prisoners pulled carts instead of carrying stones on their backs, but that wasn't a job you wanted either. The Jews were chained to the carts like a team of draught horses and whipped like animals. Only these animals were also required to sing. The Germans called them their singing horses. They had to carry a tune as they hauled enormous loads of rock up the hill. I had already been part of the prisoner chorus at Sachsenhausen. I was grateful I didn't have to do it strapped to a horse cart here.

It was only at our second roll call of the day that I saw the Buchenwald zoo.

I had seen the fenced-in area at the first roll call, but not the animals. There were deer, monkeys, even bears—bears!—right there in the concentration camp.

The zoo, I learned, was the idea of the camp's commandant, Karl Koch, and his wife, Ilse. The commandant had built it so his guards and their families would have something to entertain them. We starving prisoners stood at attention, with our hunched shoulders and gaunt faces and oversized, filthy clothes, while healthy, well-fed children and their mothers came to see the animals. The little girls wore pretty dresses and shiny black shoes and ribbons in their hair. The little boys wore shorts and jackets and caps, just as I used to. Sometimes they sucked on lollipops, watching us the way they watched the animals. What were they thinking, those little German children? Did they see animals when they looked at us, or people? I wasn't so sure myself anymore.

The bears in the zoo were fed better than the prisoners. At roll call, we'd watch as big bloody steaks were fed to the bears. I was so hungry I would have fought one of the bears for that meat and eaten it raw — steak *and* bear. One day the Nazis gave two prisoners the chance. They dropped a piece of raw meat in the mud between two men and told them to fight for it, and they did. The SS officers laughed at them and hit them with clubs while the Jews scrambled in the mud for their dinner. The animals in the zoo were never treated so badly.

The camp's commandant was a brutal man, but his wife was worse. Prisoners called her the Witch of Buchenwald and the Beast of Buchenwald. As with

Amon Goeth years before — years! — I did my best to stay away from both Herr and Frau Koch.

One day at roll call, the Witch of Buchenwald walked up and down the rows of prisoners with one of the SS guards. She came to me, checked the number tattooed on my arm, and moved to the next prisoner. She read the number tattooed on his arm and checked it against a list on a clipboard the soldier carried.

"You," she said to the prisoner. "I am told you have another tattoo."

The prisoner nodded nervously.

"Show it to me," Ilse Koch said.

The man pulled his sleeve up his thin, bony arm to show her a faded tattoo of a crescent moon.

"Yes," the witch said. "Very nice. Mark him down," she told the soldier. He made a note on his clipboard.

When they were gone, I heard the man beside me give a little whimper, like he was trying not to cry. What difference did it make that he had a tattoo? Why had it made the Witch of Buchenwald single him out? He must have been asking himself the same questions. All that mattered was that he was on the Witch's list. He had been noticed, and surviving meant never being noticed by the Nazis. After the roll call, I never saw the man with the other tattoo again.

⊷—⊷

One day I was washing myself at the camp water pump, part of my daily ritual, when I saw two SS officers lure a deer to the fence of their enclosure in the zoo. It was a sleek animal, with tall, broad antlers. While it nibbled at the food one of them offered, the other officer tied its antlers to the fence with a leather strap. The buck only discovered that it was caught when it tried to pull away. It snorted and stamped and whipped its head back and forth, trying to pull itself free, but it was trapped. The SS officers laughed at it and taunted it, and left it tied to the fence.

I had seen the Nazis do terrible things. Inhumane, unimaginably cruel things, and I had started to become numb. But somehow seeing that deer there thrashing around, trying to free itself from the fence, made my blood boil. I wanted to run over and untie it, to set it free, but I couldn't. There were too many other German soldiers around. If they saw me near the zoo I'd be shot.

So I turned my back on him. I left the buck tied to the fence. As much as I wanted to help him, I had to look out for myself.

At roll call that night, the two SS officers who had tied up the deer were pulled off duty by the commandant. Word of what they had done had gotten back to Koch, and he berated them in German. Their zoo privileges were taken away, and they were not allowed to watch films in the camp movie theater for three months.

Cruelty to prisoners the Nazis could abide. But not cruelty to animals.

—◆—

At roll call a few days later, they told us we were being moved again. Gross-Rosen needed workers, and there were no new shipments of prisoners coming in from the countryside. The prisoners in the camps would be reassigned from now on as each camp needed workers.

The Nazis had killed so many of us, they were running out of Jews.

GROSS-ROSEN
CONCENTRATION CAMP

1945

CHAPTER TWENTY-SIX

THEY TOOK US BY TRAIN. THEY PACKED US IN again, so tightly we could do nothing but stand, and gave us no food or water for the trip. People died all around me, just like before, but now I hardly took notice of it. I had been surrounded by death for so long, seen so many men die before my eyes, lived with so many dead bodies piled and stacked and strewn about like so much human firewood, that I almost couldn't care anymore. Almost. I closed my eyes on the train, trying not to see the death all around me, but I knew it was there. Sleep was my only refuge from the horror, the thirst, and the starvation, so I retreated there, dozing on again and off again as the train shuddered and creaked on its way to a new camp.

I had long since stopped hoping that each new camp would be better. Each was no better or worse than the last. They were all different rooms in purgatory, each different but each the same, and the Nazis made it all the more nonsensical by shuttling us around from one to the other, as though it made any difference.

Planes flew over the train, so low just their passing shook the cars, and we heard the patter of bullets. A bomb exploded so near the tracks we could feel the heat from it. The train stopped, and suddenly I had a vision of a bomb falling right on us, killing us all. And for a moment I wanted it to happen, the way Fred had so long ago. Anything, anything that would get me out of this nightmare.

But the planes went away and the bombs stopped falling, and the train started to move again. I couldn't have told you if I was more disappointed or relieved.

When the door to the train car finally opened at Gross-Rosen, our new concentration camp, bodies fell out. We left even more bodies in the cars. Those of us who had survived the trip, who had survived camp after camp after camp, shuffled into Gross-Rosen without fear or expectation. Nothing the Nazis could do could surprise any of us now.

They gave us our barrack assignments and put us right to bed. I sank into a deep stupor. First thing the next morning we were put to work right away, with no more time to recover from our torturous train ride like at Bergen-Belsen.

On the train, I had wanted a bomb to fall on us to put me out of my misery. But now that I was back in camp and it was the awful business as usual, my old instinct to survive kicked in again. If it was a game, then I had my own part to play; the Nazis would try to kill me, slowly, randomly, teasingly, and I would resist. I would work. I would survive. If the Nazis were going to play their game, so was I.

The Nazis had needed more workers at Gross-Rosen for the war effort. They still believed they could beat the Allies, even though we'd heard that the Russians had taken Warsaw and that Dresden was in flames.

"Any day now," prisoners whispered among one another, *"the Allies will be in Berlin, and we will be set free."*

But not today.

Today we built more barracks. As I worked, I told myself there would be another world after this one. A bright, shining, beautiful future, where I didn't wear blue and gray stripes, where I ate three full meals a day, where I wouldn't work until I passed out. Where I could have friends again. Where I could have family again. Where I could laugh again. That world existed, I knew. I couldn't reach it now, not yet, but soon. If I survived.

So I worked. Not so hard I would die, and not so little I would be punished, as Moshe had told me so long ago. I put my head down and worked, day and night, day and night. Worked to live.

"You there," a kapo said to me one day. He stopped me with the end of his club, poked into my chest. I raised my eyes to him, the first time I'd looked up in days, maybe weeks.

"Where is your button?" he asked me.

I blinked. I had no idea what he was talking about. Dully, I looked down at the ragged, dirty shirt I wore. The top button was missing. I hadn't even noticed.

"I don't know," I said. My voice surprised me. It was nothing more than a croak. I hadn't spoken a word to anyone for days. I licked my lips and tried again. "I must have lost it."

"You know what the penalty is for losing a button, don't you?" the kapo said. "Twenty lashes."

Twenty lashes. I was going to be flogged for the "crime" of losing a button. I closed my eyes. I was too tired to cry, too exhausted to even feel angry.

At roll call, I was pulled out of the lines and marched to a wooden "horse" — a polished, barkless log with four wooden feet — and laid over it with my bare back facing up.

"Keep count," the Nazi with the whip told me.

Crack! My back erupted in pain as the first lash hit me. I jerked on the log, almost falling off, but I grabbed on tighter. If I fell off, it would only be worse for me.

"One," I said in Polish.

"In German!" the soldier said. "We'll start again."

Crack! I closed my eyes to the pain. How would I ever survive twenty lashes when two hurt worse than anything I had ever felt before?

"*Eins,*" I said.

Crack!

"*Zwei.*"

Crack!

"*Drei.*"

Crack!

"*Vier.*"

Crack!

"Fuenf."

Crack!

". . . Sechs."

Crack!

". . . Sieben."

Crack!

". . . Acht."

Crack!

". . . . . . Neun."

Crack!

". . . . . . Zehn."

Crack!

". . . . . . Einzehn?"

The Nazi soldier tutted. "No, no, no. It is *elf*. Did they teach you nothing in your Jewish schools before the war? I will teach you. We'll begin again."

———

I remember very little after my lashes were finished. I couldn't even tell you how many I eventually had — many more than twenty, that was certain. When they were finished with me, I was dragged back to the barracks and dumped onto one of the shelves, where I passed out.

That night I had a dream. I was in a beautiful green

meadow. Yellow wildflowers grew here and there, so tall they swayed in the light summer's breeze. In the distance a brook burbled happily along, and a great tree beyond it spread its branches wide. I sat in the grass and listened to a cricket chirp nearby, totally at peace.

But then a dark cloud appeared on the horizon. Lightning flashed, and thunder rolled over the hills. "No," I said, not wanting my perfect afternoon disturbed. But the storm kept coming.

Lightning split the air near me, and —*krakoom!*— the thunder knocked me down. The earth shook beneath me. The ground cracked and opened. I tried to grab something to stop my fall, but my hands clutched only air. I fell into a deep, black abyss lined with tree roots and rocks, and they struck me as I fell.

Crack! Crack! Crack! Crack! Crack! I counted them in German as I fell—*eins, zwei, drei, vier, fuenf—*

Thoom!

Something exploded near the barracks, shaking me out of my dream. I raised myself up on my elbows—I had to sleep on my stomach, because my back was too raw with pain. There were prisoners packed in all around me—roll call had long since ended, and it was the middle of the night.

Thoom!

The barrack rumbled again as another bomb fell close to the camp. Everyone was awake now, every prisoner, and we watched the roof and waited without a word, waited to see if one of the bombs would fall on us and kill us all. But no. The bombs fell all through the night, and soon we all went back to sleep. Raining death was no reason not to sleep. Not when there was work to be done tomorrow.

As I laid back down on my stomach, my bloody back still screaming in agony, I remembered my dream. I told myself I would not fall down the hole. I would climb out again. The Allies were getting closer, and I was going to be there to welcome them when they got here.

DEATH MARCH

1945

CHAPTER TWENTY-SEVEN

FROM GROSS-ROSEN WE WERE TO BE MOVED again, this time to a camp called Dachau. And once more, we would walk.

It was late in the winter, almost spring, but the ground was still frozen, and the snow hadn't melted. The wooden clogs I wore were terrible for crossing icy patches and clomping through snowdrifts, but I was still better off than those who had lost their shoes, or never had any to begin with. If you could keep good care of your feet in the camps, especially on the marches, you could survive.

The sides of the road were littered with the dead bodies of Jews who had marched this way before us. They were blue and frozen, lumped into the ditches along the side of the road so cars could still pass. The bodies were a constant reminder to us to keep up the pace.

As we walked past the frozen corpses, I wondered who else used this road. Somebody else had to, surely — someone besides the German army. Who were these people who passed the bodies of dead Jews in the ditches every day on their way into town to work? How could they not see what was happening? How could they be all right with this?

Along the way, we passed through villages and sub-urbs. Little houses lined the roads, houses with painted shutters and wreaths on the doors. Electric lights lit the windows, and inside we could sometimes see a family sitting down to listen to the radio together, or washing dishes in the kitchen. Every now and then from a doorway hung a Nazi flag, bright red with a black swastika in a white circle. It was warning enough that we should keep our heads down and stay quiet as we passed through.

The route from Gross-Rosen to Dachau, north of Munich, took us through Czechoslovakia and back into Germany again. Czechoslovakia was still held by Germany — it had been one of the first countries to fall at the start of the war—but the homes we passed now were Czech, not German. Germany had conquered them, but that didn't make them love the Germans any more. If anything, the Czechs hated their Nazi overlords. There was a change in the SS officers guarding us when we crossed into Czechoslovakia. They still walked like they owned the place, but they were more wary, watching the doorways and crossroads for any sign of trouble. There were no Nazi flags to welcome them here.

No Czech revolutionaries jumped out from behind the bushes to free us, but the Czech people fought back in less violent ways. In one little village, there was bread left out on a windowsill. Bread! One of the prisoners saw it and ran for it. Others joined him, and the bread was gone before the Nazis could yell at them to stop. I saw a loaf of bread on the doorstep of another house, but it was gone before I could get it—snatched up by starving prisoners and devoured on the spot. Every Czech village we passed had some little food set out. Not nearly enough for us all, and not nearly enough for those lucky enough to get a bite to eat, but it was something.

Farther inside Czechoslovakia, some of the villagers

hung out of their windows to throw whatever they had to us—crusts of bread, half-eaten apples, raw potatoes. The Czechs couldn't share much—there was a war on, after all, and food was hard to come by. But their kindness in the face of the Nazi soldiers and their guns warmed my heart. It was easy to think the worst of humanity when all I saw was brutality and selfishness, and these people showed me there was still good in the world, even if I rarely saw it.

The kapos took as much of the food as they could for themselves, but a little still made it into the hands and mouths of the prisoners. The SS officers were mad about that, but they yelled at the Czechs, not us Jews.

"Can't you see you're helping traitors to the Fatherland?" they cried. The Czechs didn't care. Germany wasn't their fatherland, and how were we Jews traitors anyway? What had we done other than to exist?

We marched on for three days, and I still hadn't been lucky enough to get any food from the kind-hearted Czechs. I was starving, and I knew I would die of hunger before the cold got me. I was already struggling to keep ahead of the prisoners at the back of the column. Any farther back, and I would end up one of the frozen Jews on the roadside with a bullet in my head.

There was a kapo in front of me with four big loaves of Czech bread slung over his back in a cloth sack. I stared at the bread as I walked, imagining having such a feast. Four loaves! That bread would go bad before that kapo ever ate all four loaves. The kapos were healthier and better fed than the rest of us, but they were still not fed as well as the Nazis. He couldn't possibly eat that much and not get sick. What if I could talk him into giving me some? Not every kapo was a monster.

I summoned what little strength I had left and moved up closer to the kapo. I couldn't speak to him now, here, on the road. There were too many other kapos around. But maybe if I stayed close to him, made him see me as a real person, the way the Czechs saw us, maybe when I asked him tonight for bread he would take pity on me and give me some of his hoard.

I sidled up alongside the kapo, but when I saw his face I gasped.

It was Moonface.

Moonface, the kapo who had beaten me whenever he could at Bergen-Belsen. Somehow he'd been transferred to Gross-Rosen, and now he was marching south with us to Dachau.

Moonface turned and would have seen me, but I quickly backed away. What terrible luck! I wanted to cry again. So much bread, so much more bread than one person needed, and it was Moonface who held it all! Moonface would never give it to me, or to anyone else. He was too cruel.

But as I trudged along, I couldn't help staring at that sack of bread. If I didn't get food by the end of the day, I would die. I knew it. My arms shook on their own, and the green spiky leaves and toxic red berries of hollies growing alongside the road started to look appetizing. I'd be eating poisonous fruit and bark by nightfall if I didn't get some of that bread.

I marched up beside Moonface again, my hunger making me brave. What could Moonface do to me that hunger and the cold weren't already doing? I walked right alongside him until he looked down and saw me. I smiled at him, trying to make him remember me not as the boy he used to punch in the face, but as one of his best workers at Bergen-Belsen. Moonface frowned at me like he was trying to remember who I was, then ignored me.

I did everything I could to get his attention, short of talking to him. I crossed back and forth in front of him. I walked right beside him on the left and right, matching him step for step. When he walked faster, I walked faster, even though my feet were sore and frozen and my legs were so weak they wanted to quit. I wouldn't let them. Not yet.

That night we stopped in a field. I watched where Moonface went, away from the other kapos. Maybe he didn't want to share with them either. Moonface opened his sack and pulled out one of his loaves of bread, and I inched closer. I glanced around to make sure none of the other kapos were watching. If they saw me, if they heard what I was about to ask, Moonface would beat me to death. He would have to, to save face. But Moonface had sat far enough away from the other kapos that they didn't notice me. The only people around were the mute living skeletons — my fellow prisoners.

I moved close enough to stand over Moonface, and he looked up at me with his scarred, pitted, round face. I faltered. This was the face I had avoided so often at Bergen-Belsen. This was the face I had fled to Gross-Rosen to avoid. Moonface would beat me senseless for what I wanted to ask him. But what choice did I have? I cleared my throat and spoke for the first time in days.

"Do you remember me?" I croaked.

Moonface grunted and tore a bit of bread off with his teeth.

"If you remember me," I said, my voice cracking, "then you know I'm a good worker."

The other prisoners on the ground around us looked up at me with wide eyes. They must have been thinking the same thing I had, that Moonface would kill me just for talking to him. I pushed on before my courage left me.

"I—I want to work, but I won't make it on the march another day if I don't get some bread. I haven't eaten in three days, and I was—I was hoping you could give me some."

Moonface stared at me, his mouth slowly chewing on the bread like a cow working its cud.

"I—I would like to be able to work," I told him. "But I can't work without food."

Moonface laid his bread aside and pulled out a knife. He stood and put it against my throat. I tried not to flinch, but I could feel where the knife nicked my skin.

Blood from the cut ran down my neck. The prisoners around me seemed to hold their breath, waiting for me to die. Or maybe it was me holding my breath. I couldn't tell. All I could do was stand there, as tall and strong as possible, and wait for Moonface to decide my fate.

Moonface held the knife against my neck, staring into my eyes. I stared right back, showing him how strong I was, showing him I wasn't afraid to die. Neither of us blinked. Another long minute went by. If he was going to kill me, I wished he would just get it over with. I was ready to scream!

At last, Moonface pulled the knife away from my neck and I breathed again. To my amazement and to the amazement of the other prisoners watching us, Moonface cut a hunk off the loaf with his knife and tossed the bread to me. A murmur of surprise went through the prisoners around us, but Moonface silenced them with a glare. I nodded my thanks to the big ugly kapo and hurried away before he changed his mind and killed me.

My heart was racing as I found a place to lie down and eat. With shaking fingers I tore off a small piece and lifted it to my cracked lips. No bread had ever tasted so good in my life. I wanted to eat it all right then and there, but there was no telling how much farther we would have to walk. I had to save as much as I could.

Moonface had found it in his heart to be generous once, for whatever reason. But just this once.

CHAPTER TWENTY-EIGHT

WE MARCHED ANOTHER THREE DAYS BEFORE we crossed back into Germany. The Czech people continued to help us as much as they could along the way, but once we were back in Germany the doors in the villages were closed to us again, and the window shades pulled down tight. If the Germans didn't see us, they didn't have to think about us. But we left enough dead bodies in the ditches that they would know we'd been through.

I made my bread last as long as I could, but there was no way I could march for another three days. Neither could any of the other prisoners, from the looks of our ragged ranks. How close was Dachau? How much longer would it take us to get there? Would any of us be alive to see it?

The Nazis must have been thinking the same thing. On the afternoon of the sixth day, we came to a tiny depot, where a train waited for us. The kapos split us up—Jews in one train car, Poles in another—and we were loaded on. In a third car, the Nazis loaded in wooden crates.

"Our documents," one of the other prisoners told me. "They send them along with us wherever we go, the monsters. They like to keep track of who they kill and how they do it."

It seemed like an awful lot of trouble to go through for "traitors to the Fatherland."

The cattle car was crowded and unsanitary like all the rest, and there was no food or water but what we brought with us. At least we weren't walking anymore, which was a small mercy.

A day and a night passed in the train. I drifted in and out of sleep, swaying on my aching feet, but was awakened by the sound of an explosion. *Ka-boom.* It was close enough to rattle the car. Planes droned overhead. Russian? American? British? I had no idea. But they were dropping bombs all around us. *Boom. Boom. Ka-boom!* The last of them hit so close we were all thrown forward. The train's brakes screeched as it slammed to a halt, and we all struggled to look out through the slats and see what had happened. Soon word came to us from the Polish car behind us: The last car on the train had been hit with a bomb. No one had been hurt, but the car that held all our documents was destroyed.

"Ha," someone laughed humorlessly. "How will the Hitlerites know who they're killing now?"

"Easy," someone else said. "They'll know because they put all the Jews in this car, and all the Poles in that car. When we get to Dachau, they'll just gas us and put the others to work."

He was probably right. They didn't know our names anymore, but we still had our Jewish stars on our uniforms, ragged and torn though they were, and we were all in the Jewish car. As long as they kept us together, they could herd us all right into the gas chambers.

Which gave me an idea.

I found the Jewish star on my jacket. It was dirty and falling apart. Remembering my work sewing uniforms, I bit at the seams that still held it on my jacket until I could rip it off.

"They'll kill you for that," a man next to me said, watching me.

"They'll kill him for wearing it too," another man said.

I didn't listen. I had a plan. The place where the star had been sewn on was cleaner and newer-looking than anywhere else on the jacket, and you could still see the outline of the star. That would give me away for sure! I slipped my jacket off and put it on the floor, rubbing it around with my foot. When I picked it back up it was filthy all over, including the place where the star had been. Good. Now, at least, I would look the part.

When the train finally stopped outside Dachau, we were taken out of the cattle cars. As the Jews and Poles got off beside one another, I slipped from one group to the other. If the Nazis had lost our records, they wouldn't know I was a Jew unless I was standing with the Jews!

One of the Poles saw me change sides, and he frowned at me. I worked my way farther into the group and waited, my heart thumping. If I was caught, I'd be killed. I remembered how back home in Kraków, people sometimes mistook me for a Gentile. I hoped the Nazis would be fooled.

The SS officers made us line up and tell them our names and numbers.

"Prisoner B-3087," I told them. "My name is Yan Zielony." *Zielony* meant "green" in Polish. My real last name, *Gruener*, meant "greener" in German. *Zielony* made me sound more Polish, and it was easy to remember.

The Nazi wrote down my name and number and nodded me on. I had done it! I was no longer a Jew to the Nazis! I was going to live!

"That boy's a Jew," someone said. It was the man who'd seen me cross over! He pointed at me. "He came over from the other car when we got here."

The blood drained from my face. A kapo grabbed me and raised his club to hit me.

"Wait!" I cried. "I was born Jewish, but I never practiced!" I lied. "I never went to synagogue! All my friends were Poles! Christian Poles! I went to church with them! I'm not a Jew!"

"If you were born a Jew, you're a Jew," the SS officer said. He marked through my name on his sheet. "Put him with the others, where he belongs."

The kapo shoved me along to the group of watching Jews. None of them had said a word, not even the men who'd seen me take off my Star of David. When the kapo had pushed me back among my people I turned to look at the Pole who had ratted me out. He kept his eyes on the ground and wouldn't look at me. Why had he done it? What difference did it make? It's not like I would have eaten food he could have eaten or slept on a bed he could have slept on. I was nothing to him, nor him to me. And yet he had told on me when there was nothing to be gained by it. He had told on me for no other reason than that I was a Jew.

The Nazis took our names and numbers and made new documents for us to replace the ones that had been destroyed before they marched us into Dachau. They would need them so they could keep track of how they killed us all.

DACHAU
CONCENTRATION CAMP

1945

CHAPTER TWENTY-NINE

THE DAY AFTER I GOT TO DACHAU, THE MAN next to me in my bunk got the camp fever. "Camp fever" was what everyone called the typhus that spread like fire throughout the ranks of prisoners. It started with a headache and a fever, then became a cough. My bunkmate got a spotty rash on his chest, and soon he was so delirious he couldn't speak or understand a word I said to him. The Nazis did nothing to treat him, or any of the other prisoners who got the camp fever. The man from my bunk died three days later, coughing up blood. Prisoners died by the hundreds every day.

I always tried finding somewhere else to sleep, away from the sick, but it was almost impossible. More than

1,500 prisoners were crammed into barracks built to house 250 prisoners. It was a wonder we didn't all have typhus within a week, the way we had to sleep on top of one another. Each day I woke up expecting to be sick, and it seemed like a miracle when I went to bed that night, spared.

At least the Nazis didn't expect the sick to work too. They didn't make any of us work at Dachau. Prisoners had once worked here, like all the other camps, but not now. Dachau was in chaos. Some days we didn't even have roll call. The war was coming to an end, and we all knew it, even the Nazis. Like we had guessed, the Germans had been moving us around to avoid the approaching Allied attack. Even so, the chimneys still burned day and night, day and night.

One night, early in the spring, we woke in the barracks to the sound of explosions nearby. They were so close they were deafening. A building in the compound exploded, shaking our barrack, and I covered my head with my hands, just like all the prisoners around me. There was no place to go, no place to hide. The war had come to Dachau, and any moment a shell or a bomb might fall on our building and kill us all. So many times I had wished for a bomb to fall on me, to end my suffering, but now I prayed that no bomb would hit me. Not now, not when I was so close to the end! If I could survive only a little longer, I thought, just a little longer —

Planes roared overhead for hours. Bullets fired — *pop pop pop pop pop pop pop* — from inside or outside the camp, I didn't know. The heavy *poom poom poom* of artillery shook our wooden beds, and the dust and dirt of seven years rained down on us from the roof. I heard Nazis shouting to one another in German, more gunshots, more bombs exploding, but I kept my head down like the rest of the prisoners, whispering to death, pleading for it to pass me by yet again.

Then, close to dawn, the shooting and explosions stopped. I felt a rush of relief at the silence. The bullets and bombs might come again another day, but for now we were alive. Used to the sounds of war coming and going, we went back to sleep. There might be a roll call in the morning, and we would need all the rest we could get.

But come morning, something was different. For one thing, no kapo had come around to wake us up. I woke only because my body told me it was the time. As everyone stirred in their sleeping shelves, we looked around at one another, wondering where our jailers were. One of the prisoners crept to the door and peeked outside.

"There — there aren't any guards!" he told us. "I don't see any guards!"

What trick was this? I didn't believe it. Slowly we all climbed down from our shelves and looked out the windows and doors. The man was right — there wasn't a kapo or an SS officer to be seen. Prisoners staggered out of each of the barracks, looking this way and that, waiting for the Nazis to jump out and start shooting us. But the camp was empty. The Nazis had fled in the night!

I staggered into the yard, but there I stood. I didn't know what to do. None of us did. For so many years, we had only done what we were told. That was the only way to survive. Now I was on my own. I could walk right up to the front gates of the camp and walk away. But where would I go? What would I do? My home was in Kraków, hundreds of kilometers away. And what was home anymore? I had no family to go back to. No apartment that still belonged to me. I had no possessions or belongings. And even if I tried to go back, who would help me get there? Who would give me real clothes? Who would feed me? Who would be a friend to me, a Jew, when no one had stood up for me to begin with?

The grim reality set in. We were free, but we were still Jews in a land that hated us, that had stolen everything we owned and had taken our families and put us in camps and gassed us and cremated our bodies.

"Soldiers!" someone at the front gates cried. "Soldiers are coming!"

I steeled myself. So this was it then. The Nazi army would kill us all, gun us down and leave us for dead before the war ended. The extermination of the Jews was unfinished business.

Some people ran for the barracks, as if to hide, but most of them, like me, stood in the yard and waited for what was to come.

The gates opened, and soldiers marched into the yard. But the soldiers weren't wearing gray and brown. They were wearing green. Their helmets looked different from the SS helmets too. And the tank that followed them . . . the tank had an American flag on it.

"It's the Americans!" I cried, feeling something close to joy for the first time since I could remember. "The Americans are coming! The Americans!"

The Allies had reached us at last! Some prisoners hurried up to the American soldiers to shake their hands. Some hugged one another. Some gave prayers of thanks. I fell to my knees and wept. Had I really made it? Had I actually survived the Kraków ghetto and *ten* different concentration camps? I had been ten when the war started. Now I was sixteen. For more than six years I had been a prisoner of the Nazis. Prisoner B-3087. Now it was all over.

An American soldier hurried to help me up, and asked me something in English I didn't understand. He tried again in German. "What's your name?" he asked me.

"Yanek," I told him. "My name is Yanek."

"Everything's going to be all right now, Yanek," he told me, and for the first time in six years, I believed he was right.

MUNICH

1945

CHAPTER THIRTY

AS SOON AS THEY COULD, THE AMERICANS TOOK us away from Dachau. We had walked and been trucked and been taken by train so many times to so many new horrible places that some of the prisoners were reluctant to go. But the Americans assured us that all that was over, and gave us blankets and food for the short truck ride into Munich. The Allies occupied the city, and there they would house us until they figured out what to do with us.

I was put in a building that had once, I was told, been a barracks for SS officers. An American soldier led me upstairs to a big room filled with bunk beds and told me which one was mine.

"How many other people do I have to share it with?" I asked him.

He looked surprised. "Nobody," he said. "It's yours."

A bed all to myself! Then—wonder upon wonders—the soldier gave me a blanket, a pillow, and sheets for the bed. Sheets! My fellow prisoners and I looked around at one another like we were on some alien planet. I hadn't slept on a sheet, nor had a pillow or a blanket, for five years. Perhaps six.

With shaking hands, I began to make the bed. I didn't even know how, didn't remember the feeling of linens and soft things. The soldier helped me, and I climbed carefully into my new bed. A real mattress, with springs! My body sank into it, and my head fell into the pillow. What luxury!

Beside my bed there was a little table, and on the table the Americans had given me more gifts: a washcloth, a cup, and a toothbrush. I picked up the toothbrush reverently and cried as I held it in my hands. I remembered that day, standing at the pump in the camp—which camp had it been?—when I wondered when I had ever been so fortunate as to have something so simple as a toothbrush. Piece by piece, bit by bit, the Americans were giving me back my life.

That night in the dining hall, we sat in chairs. At a table. I hadn't seen a chair in six years, nor a table. The tables were long, with places set for ten people at each. The American soldiers stationed with us came in and sat down with us. We were to eat the same food the soldiers ate. There were plates at the table, and silverware. I picked up a fork and looked at it the way I had my toothbrush, like it was some artifact from another world. There were napkins too. I watched the Americans tuck their napkins into their collars and did the same.

And then they brought the food. Big platters of roast beef. Mashed potatoes. Gravy. And baskets of rolls — more bread than any of us had seen in years. The man across from me started to cry, and the American soldiers didn't know what to do.

"Would you pass the salt?" I asked him.

The man looked up at me through his tears, and he started to laugh. He was laughing and crying at the same time. "Pass the salt," he said. "Yes," he said, laughing. "Yes, let me pass you the salt."

And so we began to pass the food around, this feast the Americans had laid out for us. They couldn't understand our tears, couldn't know how amazing such a simple meal was to us. Would they ever understand? Would anyone who hadn't survived what we had survived understand? We could tell them all about it. Describe in every detail the horrors of the camps and the way we were treated. But no one who had not been there would ever truly understand.

As the food filled my plate and the soldiers and former prisoners around me began to eat, I remembered that day in Kraków so long ago, the day the war had begun. I remembered the food on the table in my old apartment in Podgórze, and all my family sitting around me. Mother and Father. Uncle Moshe and Aunt Gizela, and little cousin Zytka. Uncle Abraham and Aunt Fela. My cousins Sala, Dawid, and their two boys. They were all dead and gone now.

I thought too of my friend Fred, and the boy who had been hanged for trying to escape, and the man who had fought back, and all the other people I had watched die. They filled my table and the tables all around me, taking the places of all the real people in the room. The dead would always be with me, I knew, even when I was surrounded by life again, even if the Americans gave me back all the objects I had lost.

It would be the same for all the other prisoners too, I knew. They smiled as they ate, but there was sadness in their eyes. Sadness for the people we had lost and would never get back.

But I was wrong about losing everyone. A few days later I was out for a walk in my Munich neighborhood. I walked the streets whenever I could. I still wasn't used to the fact that I could walk as I pleased, that I wasn't gripped by thirst and hunger every second. I was thinking about what the rest of my life would hold when I saw a familiar face. She passed by on the other side of the street, and for a moment I thought I had to be mistaken.

"Mrs. Immerglick?" I called. I dashed across the street to get a closer look. "Mrs. Immerglick?"

The woman turned. It was! It was Mrs. Immerglick, the mean old lady who'd lived across the hall from me in Kraków! She burst into tears when I told her who I was, and she hugged me so hard I couldn't breathe.

"Oh, Yanek! Yanek, it is so good to see you!" she said at last. "The last time I saw you, you were just a boy! Now look at you. You're a grown man!"

I *had* grown, even in the camps. When I looked in the mirror these days, I didn't recognize the person staring back at me.

"The last time I saw you," I told her, "you yelled at me for bouncing a ball in the hall!"

"Yes! Yes! You and that ball!" She gripped my shoulders tight, as though if she let go I would disappear. "Oh, my dear boy, how I wish we could go back there now, how I wish we could start again. I wouldn't have yelled at you, I promise."

I laughed, a sound as strange to me as my own face. I hadn't laughed enough in the last six years to recognize the sound of it. "It's all right, Mrs. Immerglick. What about your boys? The rest of your family?"

"Fred," she said. Her son's name was Fred, like my friend who had died. She had tears in her eyes. "Fred survived. Like you. My Fred made it. But no one else."

I nodded, reaching out to squeeze her arm. "Is Fred here in Munich?" I asked. "I'd love to see him."

"Yes, yes. And you know about your cousin Youzek, of course."

My heart gave a small leap. "No." I was almost afraid to hope. . . .

"Oh! My dear boy! Your cousin Youzek and his wife are alive! And they're here, in Munich!"

Youzek! I hadn't seen him in years. Mrs. Immerglick brought me back to her apartment to write their address down for me on a piece of paper. I walked back out holding the paper in both hands and staring at it.

I had family—a cousin still. Family. I wasn't alone.

I went to see them as soon as I could. Cousin Youzek met me at the door, hugging me even harder than Mrs. Immerglick had. He pulled me inside and introduced me again to his wife, Hela. We cried, and laughed, and cried some more.

"How did you survive? How did you make it?" we asked each other again and again, telling our stories long into the night. Youzek and his wife had survived by hiding with friends, and they had taken in another family, the Gamzers, who had survived the same way. There were three of them: Isaac, Barbara, and little Luncia, a twelve-year-old girl who sat in the corner reading a book the whole time.

"What are your plans now, Yanek? What will you do?" Isaac Gamzer asked me as we sat around their table.

I shrugged. It was true; life had to go on. "I like movies. There's a theater near where I live now. I thought I would try to get a job as a projectionist."

"No, no, Yanek! You need to go to America!" Youzek told me. "That's where the opportunities are. That's where you can build a new life for yourself."

"America?" It felt so out of my reach now. "I don't

have any papers, any money," I replied. "How would I ever get to America?"

"There is a special program," he told me. "For Jewish orphans of the war. They will help you get your visa and pay your way."

I was instantly excited by the idea of going to America. I remembered the movies I'd watched as a boy in Kraków. Did everyone ride around on horses and wear cowboy hats? Did gangsters have shootouts in the streets? Could I really find a home there? I had to find out.

I registered for the program. I talked to lawyers. I filled out forms. I changed my name to Jacob Gruener and took to calling myself Jack, like the American soldiers called me. The process took months. Years. All the while I came back to visit Youzek and Hela almost every day, and soon I became good friends with the Gamzers too. Little Luncia and I still didn't have much to say to each other, but Isaac and Barbara became like second parents to me, even more so than Youzek and Hela. They became family.

It was hard to leave my new family when the papers finally came through in March of 1948. But I had spent years trying to get to America, and I was determined to go. Youzek, Hela, the Gamzers, and I had an emotional farewell before I boarded the train that would take me to the coast, where I would catch a ship to the United States. The Gamzers planned to come to America too, when they could, and I promised to stay in touch.

It had been almost a decade since the Nazis had rolled into Kraków. And almost that long since I'd last seen my mother and father, my uncles and aunts and other cousins. But they were gone now. I would always yearn for them and remember them, but there was nothing left for me in Europe but ghosts. I had said good-bye to all of them long, long ago.

I stepped on board the train and didn't look back. For nine years I had done everything I could to survive. Now it was time to live.

AFTERWORD

WHILE THE STORY OF JACK GRUENER IS TRUE— and remarkable—this book is a work of fiction. As an author, I've taken some liberties with time and events to paint a fuller and more representative picture of the Holocaust as a whole. All this was done with Jack's blessing so that the horrors and realities of the Holocaust beyond those that he personally experienced would not be forgotten.

Jack did, in fact, survive the harsh conditions of the Kraków ghetto by living in a pigeon coop with his parents. He baked bread under cover of night with his aunt and uncle, had his bar mitzvah in a basement, and watched his parents deported by the Nazis, never to see them alive again. At Plaszów, Jack hid under the floorboards from Amon Goeth, and was inexplicably spared by the madman when he emerged.

Even more incredibly, while Jack was at Plaszów, he worked for a time at the very same enamelware factory where German businessman Oskar Schindler later saved hundreds of Jews from extermination. Schindler was able to protect the Jews who worked there because Goeth made enough money off the factory to look the other way. But Jack was transferred away from Plaszów a mere three months before Schindler began protecting his workers from the Nazis. Jack only learned how close he was to salvation years later, when the true story of "Schindler's List" was told.

Jack then went on to survive nine more concentration camps. At Wieliczka, he toiled beside the famous salt statues that became a tourist attraction after the war. At Birkenau, he waited under the gas heads for death, only to be showered with cold water instead. At Auschwitz, Jack came face-to-face with the infamous Nazi monster Josef Mengele and lived. Jack endured slavery and starvation, death marches and cattle cars, Allied bombings and Nazi beatings. Of the more than one and a half million Jewish children living in Europe before the war, Jack was one of only a half million to survive.

After the war, Jack immigrated to America and became an American citizen. Less than a year after he became a citizen, he was drafted into the U.S. Army and sent to Korea to fight in the Korean War. There he survived again—this time with a gun in his hands and a pack on his back—all the while keeping up his promised correspondence with the Gamzer family, who had at last immigrated to America.

When Jack's two years in the army were up, he came to visit the Gamzers in New York City. He discovered that little Luncia, the girl he had met in Munich who always sat in the corner reading a book, had grown up into a beautiful young woman. Jack fell in love with Luncia—who had since changed her name to Ruth—and in a few months they were married.

Jack and Ruth now live in Brooklyn, New York. They have two grown sons and four grandchildren. Together, Jack and Ruth travel the country to speak about their experiences in the Holocaust. I had the pleasure of meeting Jack and Ruth while working on this book, and it is my honor to write about Jack's life so the generations that follow will never forget. Jack still bears the tattoo with the number the Nazis gave him—*B-3087*—but it is *his* name, Jack Gruener, that lives on.